SUICIDE MISSION

Three desperate men find themselves behind bars in a wild and leaderless country still seething with the slaughter and bloodshed of revolution.

The first is Emmet Keogh, a tough little fugitive from his native Ireland, a former IRA terrorist who began killing as a teenager and hasn't stopped since.

The second is Oliver van Horne, an enigmatic giant masquerading as a priest. Before his capture he toted a Thompson submachine gun beneath his cassock, and $50,000 in cash he had liberated from an American bank.

The third is Janos, ex-member of the Austrian Imperial guard, now a hotelkeeper and a whisky smuggler and gunrunner extraordinaire.

Lonely, bitter, and due to be hanged, they are offered their lives if they can put an end to a murderous renegade who commands a small army and brutally holds an entire province in thrall.

The Wrath of God

JAMES GRAHAM

A DELL BOOK

For David Godfrey with thanks

Published by
DELL PUBLISHING CO., INC.
1 Dag Hammarskjold Plaza
New York, N.Y. 10017

ISBN: 0-440-18824-5

Reprinted by arrangement with Doubleday & Company, Inc.
Printed in the United States of America
Previous Dell Edition #8824
New Dell Edition
First printing—July 1978

MEXICO
1922

ONE

The Chief of Police usually managed to execute somebody round about noon on most days of the week, just to encourage the rest of the population, which gives a fair idea of how things were in that part of Mexico at the time.

The sound of the first ragged volley sent my hand down inside my coat in a kind of reflex action when I was half-way up the hill from the railway station. For most of the way I had managed to stay in the shade, but when I emerged into the Plaza Cívica, the sun caught me by the throat and squeezed hard, bringing sweat from every pore.

The executions were taking place in the courtyard of the police barracks and the gates stood wide open to give an uninterrupted view to anyone interested enough to watch, which on that occasion meant a couple of dozen Indians and mestizos. Not a bad audience considering the noonday heat and the frequency with which the performance was repeated.

At the rear of the small crowd, an automobile was parked, a Mercedes roadster with the hood down, the entire vehicle coated with a layer of fine white dust from the dirt roads. An exotic item to find in a town like Bonito at that time. More surprising was the driver who was getting out just as I arrived, for he was a

priest, although like no other priest I'd seen outside
of Ireland—a great ox of a man in a shovel hat and
faded cassock.

He ignored the rest of the audience, most of whom
were surprised to see him there, produced a cigarillo
from a fat leather case and searched for a match.
I found one before he did, struck it and held it out for
him.

He turned and looked at me sharply, giving me a
sight of his face for the first time. A tangled greying
beard, vivid blue eyes and the unmistakable furrow
of an old bullet wound along the side of his skull just
above the left eye. One of the lucky ones to survive the
Revolution.

He took the light without a word and we stood side-
by-side and watched as they marched three Indians
across the courtyard from the jail and stood them
against the wall. There were already half-a-dozen bodies on the ground and the wall was pitted with scars.
The three men stood there impassively as a sergeant
tied their hands behind their backs.

The priest said, "Does this happen often?"

He had spoken in Spanish, but with an accent that
indicated that he was anything but Mexican.

I replied in English, "The Chief of Police says it's
the only way he can keep down the numbers in the
jail."

He glanced at me with a slight frown. "Irish?"

"As ever was, Father."

"A long way from home."

*New England American, or somewhere near unless
I missed my guess.*

"I thought the Revolution was supposed to be over?"
he said, and looked back towards the scene in the
courtyard. "What a bloody country."

Which was a reasonably unpriestlike remark although understandable in the circumstances. I said, "The discontented are always with us, Father, even after revolutions. Why, there are some in these parts who think it's still open season on priests."

"We're in God's hands," he said harshly. "All of us."

Which was arguable, but I was prevented from taking the question up with him for one of the condemned against the wall inside the courtyard cried out sharply and pointed to us as the sergeant was about to tie his hands.

There was some kind of disturbance and then a young officer strolled in the direction of the gate and beckoned to the priest, who left me without a word and went towards him.

"Believe it or not, Father, but one of these pigs wants to confess," I heard the officer say.

The priest said nothing; simply took a breviary from his pocket, spat out his cigarillo and started through the gate. By the time he reached the wall, all three were on their knees waiting for him.

I didn't stop to watch for I had seen men die before or at least that's what I told myself as I turned and went across the square to the Hotel Blanco on the far side. It was a tall slender building, which had been used as a strongpoint by the government forces during the war, and the crumbling façade was pitted with bullet holes.

In the patio a fountain splashed water across scarlet tiles and the cool darkness of the terrace looked very inviting. The owner of the place lounged in a wicker chair by the screen door, fanning himself with a palm fan. His name was Janos and he was Hungarian as far as I could make out, although his English was excellent. The most noticeable thing about him was his great size. He must have been seventeen or eighteen stone at least, with a great pendulous belly, and sweated constantly.

"Ah, Mr. Keogh. A hot day. You will join me in a beer?"

There were several stone bottles of lager in a bucket of water at his side. I helped myself to one and pulled the cork. As I did so, another volley sounded in the courtyard opposite. I sat on the rail beside him as the crowd began to disperse.

"A nasty business," Janos said, managing to sound as if he didn't give a damn.

"Yes, too bad," I answered automatically, for I was watching for the priest.

He emerged from the gateway with the officer, who walked to the Mercedes with him. They stood talking for a while, then the officer saluted and the priest got into the car and drove away.

"A strange sight, that." Janos commented. "Not only a priest, but a priest in an automobile."

"I suppose so." I emptied the beer bottle and stood up.

"But not to you, Mr. Keogh. Here, have another beer." He lifted one, dripping wet from the bucket and held it out to me. "In your Ireland you will have been familiar with such vehicles. Here, they are still a rarity. You can drive yourself, I understand?"

Which was leading to something. I said, "It's not very difficult."

"For an intelligent man, perhaps not, but these peasants." He shrugged. "They are incapable of learning anything beyond the simplest tasks. I myself have a truck. The only one in Bonito. Most important to my business. I imported a driver mechanic specially from

Tampico, but the wretched man had to go and involve himself in politics."

"A dangerous thing to do in this country."

He wiped a fresh layer of sweat from his fat face. "He was in the first batch they shot this morning. Most unfortunate."

He obviously meant for himself personally. I said, "That's life, Mr. Janos. He shouldn't have joined."

A pretty hard way of looking at it, but then most of the more human feelings had been burned out of me a long time ago, particularly where that kind of situation was concerned. It was none of my affair and I was tired of the conversation which for some reason had a strange air of unreality to it. I was hot and I was tired and wanted nothing so much as a bath and perhaps a couple of hours on my bed before the train left.

I stood up and Janos said, "I have a rather important consignment to go to Huila. You know the place, perhaps?"

I saw then what he wanted, but there was no reason why I should make it easy for him. "No, I can't say I do."

"Two hundred miles north of here toward the American border. Dirt roads, but not too bad in the dry season."

But by then, I'd had enough. I said, "I'm catching the two-thirty train for Tampico."

"You could be back by tomorrow night. Catch the train the following day."

"But miss the boat to Havana tomorrow evening." I said, "And there's no refund on the ticket."

"How much was it? Forty-two American dollars?" He shrugged. "I will pay you five hundred, Mr. Keogh. Five hundred good American dollars and very easily earned, you must admit."

Which brought me up rather sharply because after paying for my tickets I'd no more than twenty or thirty dollars left.

"That's a great deal of money for running a few supplies up country," I said carefully.

So he decided to be honest with me, the great shining face creasing into a jovial man-to-man smile. "I will be frank with you, Mr. Keogh. The crates in my truck contain good scotch whisky. A commodity in short supply in Mexico, God alone knows, but over the border they have what is known as Prohibition. There it will be worth considerably more."

"Including a five-year prison sentence if you're caught running the stuff," I pointed out.

"A risk someone else assumes," he said. "The man who takes over the consignment in Huila. You, my friend, will be breaking no law known to me. Not while you are in Mexico. To trade in alcohol here is perfectly legitimate."

Which was true enough and the prospect was tempting for even if I forfeited that boat ticket I'd still be considerably better off.

He thought he had me and gave it another push. "I'll tell you what I'll do, Mr. Keogh. Five hundred and another boat ticket. Now can I say fairer, sir? Answer me that."

He was being jovial again, which didn't become him, but his eyes, those sad, grey, Hungarian eyes were still and watchful and I think it was that which really decided me, combined with the fact that I wasn't at all sure that I liked him.

"No thanks," I said. "The price is too high."

The smile was wiped clean, the eyes became totally blank. "I don't understand you. I know your financial situation. What you say doesn't make sense."

"It wouldn't," I said. "I wasn't talking about money, Mr. Janos. I was talking about Mexico. I've had all I can take. Six months of heat, flies and squalor. And I haven't known a day when they haven't been shooting somebody. You'll have to find someone else."

"I don't think you understand," he said carefully. "There is no one else."

"Which is your problem, not mine."

The palm fan had stopped moving and he sat there staring at me and yet not at me, sweat pouring down his face, those gray eyes fixed on a point somewhere beyond me. The fan started to move again, rapidly, and he wiped the sweat away with his enormous silk handkerchief.

And suddenly that jovial smile was back in place. "Why then, I can only wish you luck, sir, and shake you by the hand."

He held it out and I took it for it would have seemed churlish not to, but it was the wrong kind of grip for a fat man who did nothing but sit and sweat. Firm and strong—very strong, which made me feel distinctly uneasy as I walked away for he had given in too easily.

Before the Revolution the Hotel Blanco must have been rather spectacular, but now there were cracks on the marble stairs, great slabs of plaster flaking away from the walls. It was as if the place were disintegrating slowly. There was no lock on my door, which always stood open a little, and inside the room was like an oven for the electric fan in the ceiling hadn't turned for five years, which was when they'd dynamited the power plant.

I managed to get the shutters open, breaking a couple of slats in the process, and let in a little warm air. I was soaked in sweat and the revolver in the leather shoulder holster under my right arm had rubbed painfully. I took off my jacket, unstrapped the holster, with some relief, and put it down on the bed.

Once this room had been something quite special for it still had its own bathroom through the far door, but now it had that derelict air common to cheap rooms the world over. It was as if no one had ever really lived here. For no accountable reason I ached for some soft Kerry rain on my face again. Wanted to stand with my eyes turned up to it, to let it run into my mouth, but that was not to be. That was foolishness of the worst kind.

The bathroom had the same air of tarnished magnificence as the rest of the hotel. The floor and the walls were covered with imported Italian tiles, all sporting little naked cherubs offering bunches of grapes to each other. The bath itself was cracked in a hundred places, but big enough to swim in and, although most of the brass fittings had been stolen at one time or another, tepid brown water still gushed from a gilded lion's mouth when you turned the handle.

I returned to the bedroom, took off the rest of my clothes and pulled on my old robe. Then I went back into the bathroom, taking the shoulder holster with me for old habits die hard.

The water was by now so brown that I was unable to see the bottom of the bath, but I lowered myself in without a qualm and lay back and stared up at the cracked ceiling.

How easily things become what we want them to. The cracks on that ceiling became a map, line by line flowering into shape before me. The railway snaking down through Monterrey to Tampico. Then the route across the Gulf north of the Yucatán Peninsula to Cuba and Havana town.

And what would I do there? I had an address, no more than that. A man who might be able to give me work or might not. And afterwards? But there was no answer to that one and each day would have to bring what it chose.

There was a sudden muffled crash from the bedroom that had me out of the bath and reaching for my revolver all in the same moment. I flattened myself against the wall beside the door, out of the line of fire if anyone intended to shoot their way in.

I got my robe on one-handed and not without difficulty and listened. There was no sound, so I did what seemed the obvious thing, flung open the door and dropped to one knee.

The man who stood by the bed searching my jacket was straight out of the market place, a mestizo in ragged trousers and shirt and palm leaf sombrero. He had just taken the wallet from the inner pocket. Everything I had in the world.

"Not today, *compadre*," I said. "Put it on the bed and quickly."

At first it looked as if he was going to do as he was told. His shoulders sagged. He said brokenly, "Señor, my wife, my children. For pity's sake."

Which didn't particularly impress me for any painter specializing in theological subjects would have found him a fair likeness for Judas Iscariot. It worked to a certain degree for when he turned to fling the jacket in my face and ran, he definitely caught me off balance.

When I reached the door, he was almost at the head of the stairs, which didn't give me a great deal of choice as he was still clutching my wallet in his right hand, so I brought him down with a snap shot in the right leg.

He went over the edge of the stairs without a cry and I heard him crash against the ironwork banisters twice. When I reached the head of the stairs he was lying facedown on the next landing. He glanced back over his shoulder, his face twisted with rage and to my complete astonishment, started to slither down the rest of the broad marble stairs leaving a snail's trail of blood behind him.

Several things happened at about the same time then. Janos came stumping out of the shadows leaning on his black ivory walking stick, a couple of retainers from the kitchen at his back. "By God, sir, what's going on here?"

"My wallet," I said. "He stole my wallet."

The thief slid the rest of the way down to the hall and collapsed at the fat man's feet. Janos leaned over him and poked around in the shadows. When he straightened, his face was grave and baleful.

"Wallet, sir? I see no wallet here."

Which was when my heart really started to sink as it suddenly occurred to me that there was just a faint possibility that there was more to this than met the eye.

The police arrived on the run, armed to the teeth as usual, ready to spray everything in sight as they came through the door, although the sergeant in charge was exquisitely polite and listened to my story with the utmost patience.

The wretch on the floor, whom no one seemed to be particularly concerned about, clutched his leg, blood oozing between his fingers and cursed all gringos and their seed to the tenth generation. He was wholly innocent and employed by Señor Janos as a general porter. The sergeant booted him casually in the ribs, left his men to search for the wallet and took me up to my room to get dressed.

"Do not worry, señor," he comforted me. "The man is a known thief. Señor Janos gave him honest work out of the largeness of his heart and this is how he serves him. We will find this wallet. Fear not, your name will be cleared."

But when he returned to the foot of the stairs and he discovered his men's lack of success, a fact to which I had already become resigned, his face assumed a more melancholy expression.

"This is a grave matter, señor, you realise my position? To shoot this man for stealing your wallet is one thing . . ."

"But to shoot him, full stop, is quite another."

"Exactly, señor, I am afraid you must accompany me to headquarters. The *jefe* himself will wish to question you."

His hand on my arm was no longer gentle and as we moved forward, Janos said passionately, his jowls shaking, "By God, sir, I'll stand by you. Trust in me, Mr. Keogh."

Hardly the most comforting of thoughts on which to be led away.

Above the town the Sierras floated in a blue haze, marching north toward the border. It was all I could see when I hauled myself up by the iron bars on the narrow window and peered out.

I was in what was known as the general reception cell, a room about forty feet square with rough stone walls that looked as if they might very well pre-date Cortez. There were about thirty of us which meant it was pretty crowded and the smell seemed compounded

of urine, excrement and human sweat in equal pro-
portions.

An hour of this was an hour too much. An *indio* got
up and relieved himself into an overflowing bucket
and I moved out of the way hurriedly, took a packet
of Artistas out of my pocket and lit one.

Most of the others were *indios* with flat, impassive
brown faces, simple men from the back country who'd
come to town looking for work and now found themselves in prison and probably for no good reason
known to man.

They watched me out of interest and curiosity because I was the only European there, which was a very
strange thing. One of them stood up from the bench
on which he sat, removing his straw sombrero and
offered me his seat with a grave peasant courtesy that
meant I couldn't possibly refuse.

I sat down, took out the packet of Artistas and offered them around and hesitantly, politely, those
closest to me took one and soon we were all smoking
amicably, the lighted cigarettes passing from mouth
to mouth.

The bolt rattled in the door which opened to re-
veal the sergeant. "Señor Keogh, please to come this
way."

So we were being polite again? I followed him out
and along the whitewashed corridor as the door
clanged behind me. We went up the steps into a sweet-
er, cleaner world and crossed towards the administra-
tion block of the police barracks.

I had been here once before about four months pre-
viously to obtain a work permit and had been required
to pay through the nose for it, which meant that the
jefe in Bonito was about as honest as the usual run of
police chiefs.

The sergeant left me on a bench in a whitewashed corridor under the eye of two very military-looking guards who stood on either side of the *jefe's* door clutching Mannlicher rifles of the type used by the Germans in the war. They ignored me completely and after a while the door opened and the sergeant beckoned.

The room was sparsely furnished, desk, filing cabinet and not much else, except for a couple of chairs, one of which was occupied by my fat friend from the Hotel Blanco, the other by the *jefe*.

Janos lurched to his feet and swayed there, propped up by his ivory stick, sweat shining on his troubled face. "A dreadful business, Mr. Keogh, but I'm with you, sir, all the way."

He subsided again. The *jefe* said, "I am José Ortiz, Chief of Police in Bonito, Señor Keogh. Let me first apologise for your treatment so far. A regrettable error on the part of my sergeant here who will naturally answer for it."

The sergeant didn't seem to be worrying too much about that and the *jefe* opened a file before him and studied it. He was a small, olive-skinned man in his fifties with a carefully trimmed moustache and most of his teeth had been capped with gold.

He looked up at me gravely. "A most puzzling affair, Señor Keogh. You say this man was stealing your wallet?"

"That's right."

"Then what has he done with it, senor? We have searched the stairs and the foyer of the hotel thoroughly."

"Perhaps he had an accomplice," I suggested. "There were several people milling around there."

"By God, he could be right," Janos cut in. "It could explain the whole thing."

The *jefe* nodded. "Yes, that is certainly a possibility and on the whole, I am inclined to believe your story, señor, for the man is a known thief."

"That is very kind of you," I said gravely.

"There was much in the wallet of importance?"

"Twenty or thirty dollars, some rail and steamer tickets and my passport."

He raised his eyebrows. "So? Now that is serious. More so than I had realised." He looked in the file again. "I see from your papers that you were registered as a British citizen. This is correct?"

I said calmly, "That's right."

"Strange. I thought you Irish had your Free State now since the successful termination of your revolution."

"Some people might question that fact," I told him.

He seemed puzzled, then nodded brightly. "Ah, but of course, now you have your civil war. The Irish who fought the English together now kill each other. Here in Mexico we have had the same trouble." He glanced at the file again. "So you would be able to obtain a fresh passport from the British Consul in Tampico."

"I suppose so."

He nodded. "But that will take some weeks, señor, and what are we to do with you in the meantime. I understand you are not at present employed."

"No, I worked for the Hermosa Mining Company for six months."

"Who have now, alas, suspended operations. I foresee a difficulty here."

"Oh, I don't know," I said. "I'm sure Mr. Janos can suggest something."

"By God, I can, sir," he said, stamping his stick on

the floor. "I've offered Mr. Keogh lucrative employ-ment—highly lucrative. For as long as he likes."

Ortiz looked relieved. It was really a quite excellent performance. "Then everything is solved, Señor Keogh. If Señor Janos makes himself personally responsible for you, if I have this guarantee that you will be in secure employment, then I can release you."

"Was there ever any question of it?" I asked politely.

He smiled, closed the file, got to his feet and held out his hand. "At your service, Señor Keogh."

"At yours, señor," I replied punctiliously, turned and went out.

I heard a quiet, murmured exchange between them and then Janos stumped after me. "All's well that ends well, eh, Mr. Keogh? And I'll stick to my bargain, sir. I shan't take advantage of your situation. Five hundred dollars and your steamer ticket. That's what I said and that's what I'll pay."

"A gentleman," I said. "Anyone can see that."

His great body shook with laughter. "By God, sir, we'll deal famously together. Famously."

A matter of opinion, but then all things were possible in that worst of all possible worlds.

TWO

When we got back to the hotel, Janos took me round to the stables in the rear courtyard. A couple of stalls had been knocked out at one end and the truck stood in there.

It was a Ford and looked as if it had spent a hard war at the Western Front. There was a canvas tilt at the back and it was loaded to the roof with medium-sized packing cases. I checked the wheels and discovered that the tyres were new, which was something, then I lifted the bonnet and had a look at the engine. It was in better shape than I could have reasonably hoped.

"You find everything in order?" he demanded.

"You lost a good mechanic this morning."

"Yes, an inconvenience, but much of life generally is."

"When do you want me to go?"

"If you left now, you could make the half-way point by dark. There is an inn at Huerta. A poor place, but adequate. It was a way-station in the old stage coach days. You could spend the night there. Be at Huila before noon tomorrow. This suits you?"

Amazing how polite he was being about it all. "Absolutely," I said, but the irony in my voice seemed to elude him.

"Good," he nodded in satisfaction. "Let's go in and I'll give you the final details."

His office was just off the patio at the front of the building, a small cluttered room with a polished oak desk and a surprising number of books. My shoulder holster and the Enfield were lying on the desk and he tapped them with the end of his stick.

"You'll be wanting that, I've no doubt. Rough country out there these days."

I took off my jacket and buckled on the holster. He said, "You look uncommonly used to that contrivance, sir, for a man of your obvious education and background."

"I am," I told him shortly and pulled on my jacket. "Anything else?"

He opened a drawer, took out two envelopes and pushed them across. "One of those is a letter to Gomez, the man to whom you'll deliver the goods in Huila. He has a supply of petrol by the way, so you'll be all right for the return trip. The other contains an authorisation to make the journey signed by Captain Ortiz, in case you are stopped by *rurales*."

I put them both in my breast pocket and buttoned my jacket. He selected a long black cigar from a sandalwood box, lit it, then pushed the box across to me. "You'll have a drink with me, sir, for the road?"

"We have a saying where I come from," I told him. "Drink with the devil and smile."

He laughed till the tears squeezed from his eyes, the flesh trembling on the gross body. "By God, sir, but you're a man after my own heart, I can see that."

He shuffled across to a side cabinet, opened it and produced a bottle and a couple of tumblers. It was brandy and good brandy at that.

He leaned one elbow on the cabinet and eyed me

gravely. "If I might be permitted the observation, sir, you don't seem to care very much about anything. About anything at all. Am I right?"

That strange, rather pedantic English of his had a curious effect. It made one want to respond in kind. I said, "Why, it has been my experience that there is little in life worth caring about, sir."

I could have sworn that for a moment there was genuine concern in his eyes although I considered it unlikely he could ever have afforded such an emotion.

"If I may say so," he observed heavily, "I find such sentiments disturbing in one so young."

But now, the conversation had gone too far and we were into entirely the wrong territory. I emptied my glass and placed it carefully down on top of the cabinet. "I'd better be on my way."

"Of course, but you'll need a little eating money." He produced a wallet and counted out a hundred pesos in ten peso notes. "You should be back here by tomorrow evening if everything goes smoothly."

By now he was looking quite pleased with himself again, which simply wouldn't do. I stuffed the money carelessly into my jacket pocket and said, "Life has taught me one thing above all others, Mr. Janos, which is that anything can happen and usually does."

His face sagged in genuine and immediate dismay for as I discovered later, there was a strongly superstitious streak in him, his one great weakness. I laughed out loud, turned and walked out. A small victory, perhaps, but something.

I was eighteen years of age when I first saw men die. Easter, 1916, and a sizable section of Dublin town going up in flames as a handful of volunteers decided to have a crack at the British Army.

And I was one of them, Emmet Keogh, hot from my books at the College of Surgeons, still young enough to believe a cause—any cause—could be worth the dying. A Martini carbine gripped tightly in my hands, I sweated in ill-fitting green uniform and crouched at the window of an office in Jacobs' Biscuit Factory, a romantic place to die in, waiting for the Tommies from the Portobello Barracks to find us, which they did soon enough.

During a slight lull in the proceedings, a Mills bomb came through the window and rolled to a halt in the very centre of that busy office.

There were six of us in there who should have died, but for some reason it didn't go off until I'd thrown it back out of the window at the troops who had chosen that precise moment to make a rush across the yard.

Life, then, or death, was an accident one way or the other. Time and chance and no more than that. Let it be so. Certainly from that day on it conditioned not only my actions, but my thinking. Janos had been closer to the truth about me than he knew.

For the first few miles out of Bonito the road wasn't too bad, in fact had obviously been metalled at some time in the past, but not for long. Soon it changed into a typical back-country dirt road with a surface so appalling that it was impossible to drive at more than twenty-five miles an hour in any kind of safety.

In the distance, the Sierras undulated in the intense heat of late afternoon and as I drove towards them but slightly to the north-west, a great cloud of white dust rising from the loose surface coated everything including me.

A flat brown plain stretched on either hand as far as the eye could see, dotted with thorn bushes and mesquite and acacias. I was alone on a road that led to nowhere through a land squeezed dry by the sun, barren since the beginning of time.

God, but there were times when I ached for my own country, for the sea and the mountains of Kerry, green grass, soft rain and the fuchsia growing on dusty hedges. The Tears of God we called it.

I passed nothing that lived for the first hour, then a dot in the far distance grew into a herd of goats, an old man and two young boys in charge, barefooted, ragged, so wretchedly poor that even their straw sombreros were falling to pieces. They stood watching me, faces blank, making no sign at all, the sullen despair of those truly without hope.

I stopped a mile or two further on to get rid of my jacket, being well soaked with sweat by then and drank and sluiced my head and shoulders with lukewarm water from a four-gallon stone jug someone had thoughtfully roped into place in front of the passenger seat.

From there on things became so bad that I had to drive very cautiously indeed, sometimes at not more than ten or fifteen miles an hour and the heat and the dust were unbelievable. I had been on the road for three and a half hours, had seen no one except the goatherds, was beginning to believe I was the only living thing in this sterile world when I found the priest.

The Mercedes was a little way off the road and had ploughed its way through a clump of organ cactus. The priest stood at the side of the road, his cassock and broad-brimmed hat coated with dust and waved me down. I braked to a halt and got out.

He recognised me at once and smiled. "Ah, my Irish friend."

His front near-side tyre had burst, which explained his sudden departure from the road, but he had come to rest with his rear axle jammed across a sizable rock and had spent a futile hour trying to push the car free.

The solution was ludicrously simple. I said, "If we raise her off the rock with the jack and give her a good push she should roll clear soon enough."

"Why damn my eyes," he said. "Why didn't I think of that?"

He would have gone down well on the Dublin Docks, but I didn't say so. Simply opened his boot, which was full of five-gallon cans of petrol, got out the jack and started to work.

"No reason why I shouldn't do that, it seems to me," but he didn't try too hard to dissuade me, lit one of those long, black cigarillos he favoured and stood watching. I was sweating hard and the shoulder holster was something of a nuisance so I unstrapped it and put it on the rear seat of the Mercedes. Chancing to glance up a moment later, I saw that he was holding the Enfield in his right hand.

"Careful, Father," I warned. "What's known in the trade as a hair trigger. She'll go off at a breath."

"Wouldn't it be better to have the pin fall on an empty chamber for the first pull," he suggested. "In case of accidents?"

Which was reasonably knowledgeable for a man of the cloth. "Fine, if you have the time to waste."

"Presumably you don't."

"Not very often."

He stood there, still holding the Enfield in one hand, the holster in the other. "You were out in the Troubles," he said. "Against the English, I mean?"

It was the kind of language American newspapers had been fond of at the time. I nodded. "You could say that."

"This Civil War back there is a bad business." He

shook his head. "From what I read in the papers the Irish are killing each other off more savagely these days than the English ever did. Why, didn't Republican gunmen kill Michael Collins himself only three or four months ago, and I always understood he did more to beat the English than any man."

"Then settled for half-a-loaf," I said. "Not good enough."

"A die-hard Republican, I see." He hefted the Enfield in his hand and said, "Not that I know about such things, but it doesn't feel very comfortable."

"It wouldn't," I told him. "I'm left-handed. The grip has been altered to fit."

He examined the gun further, obviously intrigued by the absence of a sight at the end of the blue-black barrel, the way most of the trigger guard had been cut away. I concentrated on the jack lever and as the axle started to clear, he dropped the shoulder holster inside the Mercedes, hitched up his cassock and got to his knees beside me.

"What do you think?"

"Put your shoulder to the boot and we'll find out."

It took the two of us, and some considerable effort. There was a moment when I thought it wasn't going to go and then the jack tilted forward and the Mercedes rolled free, scraping the rear bumper on the rock in the process. He lost his balance and fell on his hands and knees and I ran around and got the handbrake on before the Mercedes got clear away from us. When I turned, he was getting to his feet, rubbing dust from his beard and grinning like a schoolboy.

"A hell of a way to spend an afternoon."

"I could think of pleasanter things to do," I admitted. "In more comfortable places." I stretched my aching back and looked out across the wilderness. "The last place God made."

He was about to light another of his cigarillos and paused, the match flaring in his right hand, his face grave and somehow expectant. "At least you give him some credence, even for this."

"In a place like this it's difficult to say God doesn't exist, Father." I shrugged. "Try, and he'll more than likely remind you of his presence rather forcibly."

"Something of an Old Testament view of things, I would have thought," he said. "A God of wrath, not of love."

"A view of the Almighty my own experience would tend to support," I said flatly.

He nodded, his face grave, "Yes, life can be very hard. It's difficult to live each day as an act of faith. I know, I've been trying for forty-nine years, but it's the only way."

I picked up the jack, went round to the front of the Mercedes and set to work. He was carrying two spare wheels, a wise precaution in such country and the changeover took me no more than five minutes. He didn't offer to help, didn't try to carry our conversation any further, but walked some little distance away to a slight rise where he stood looking out at the mountains.

When I called, he didn't seem to hear me and I went towards him, cleaning my hands on an old rag. As I got closer, he turned and said harshly, "Yes, my friend, you're right. In a place like this it must be difficult to believe in anything."

But I was no longer interested in that kind of conversation. "I think everything's all right now," I said. "Drive her back to the road and we'll see."

The Mercedes had a self-starter and the engine

turned with no trouble at all, a change from most of
the vehicles I'd had experience with. I jumped on the
running-board and he took her round in a wide circle,
joining the road a few yards behind the Ford.

I got my shoulder holster and the Enfield from the
rear seat and buckled them on. "You see, Father, everything comes out in the wash if only you live right."

He laughed, switched off the engine and held out
his hand. "Young man, I like you, damn me if I don't.
My name is van Horne. Father Oliver van Horne of
Altoona, Vermont."

"Keogh," I said. "Emmet Keogh. Catholic priests
who've been shot in the head must be rather thin on
the ground in Vermont."

His hand went to the scar on his temple instinctively. "True enough, but then I was the only one to my
knowledge, who served as chaplain to an infantry bri-
gade on the Western Front."

"Aren't you rather far from home?"

"I'm on a general fact-finding trip on behalf of my
diocesan authorities. We understood that in the back
country in Mexico the Church has been in great difficulties since the Revolution. I'm here to see what
help is needed."

"Look, Father," I said. "I wasn't joking this morning in Bonito when I told you there were people in
these parts who thought it was still open season on
priests. I know places where they haven't seen one in
years and don't want to. Last month in Hermosa a
young French priest tried to re-open the church after
eight years. They hung him from the verandah of the
local hotel. I saw him swinging."

"And did nothing?"

"I've seen priests who stood by and did nothing in
my own country," I said. "It's easy to take the last walk

with a prayer book in your hand when someone else is going to do the dying. Damned hard to stand up and fight for what you believe in against odds."

For some reason I was angry, which was illogical in the circumstances and I think I knew it. In any event, I went round to the front of the Ford and turned the starting handle. As the engine jumped into life, van Horne joined me.

"I seem to have annoyed you," he said. "And for that I'm sorry. A shocking tendency to preach on each and every occasion is my besetting sin. I'm hoping to make my way through the Sierras to a place called Guayamas on the west coast. What about you?"

"Delivering a load of bootleg whisky to a man in Huila," I said. "You'll find petrol there if you're short."

"Do you hope to get there tonight?"

I shook my head. "There's a little place called Huerta about twenty miles further on. Old stage line way-station."

"Perhaps I'll see you there."

I smiled and climbed into the cab of the Ford. "If you do, for God's sake keep religion out of it, Father."

"Almost impossible," he said. "But I'll do what I can. God bless you."

But sentiments like those had long since ceased to have any effect on me and I drove away quickly.

Suddenly, it seemed to be late evening, the sun dropping behind the Sierras taking the heat of the day with it, the great peaks black against gold as the fire died. There was no sign of the Mercedes coming up behind and I wondered what he was doing. A strange one certainly, although priests, like anyone else, were entitled to their idiosyncrasies.

I came over the brow of a small hill just before dark and saw the way-station at Huerta lying below me, lights winking palely at the windows. It was a small, flat-roofed building, which must have been a hundred and fifty years old at least, and was enclosed by an adobe wall, most of which had crumbled away where the place faced the road.

The sky beyond was like molten gold, the great black fingers of the organ cactuslike cut-outs pasted in place against a stage set as I coasted down the hill. When I turned in across the courtyard and switched off the engine, I heard laughter and singing and there were half-a-dozen horses tied to the hitching post. The door opened as I got out and a man appeared, bare-headed, a couple of bandoleers criss-crossing his ornate jacket, a rifle in his hands.

"Stand and declare yourself," he called and his speech was slurred with the drink.

I could have shot him, been back behind the wheel of the Ford and away before his friends inside knew what was happening, but there was no need, for I had already noticed the large silver badge so conspicuously displayed on his right breast, worn only by the *rurales,* the country police, as fine a body of men who ever cut a throat or raped a woman and got away with it.

"I'm taking supplies to Gomez in Huila," I said. "I have a permit from Captain Ortiz, the *jefe* in Bonito."

"Inside," he said, "where we can see you."

The place was lit by a single oil lamp hanging from one of the beams in the low ceiling. There were four of them sitting at a long wooden table, two holding pistols at the ready as I went in. They wore the same ornate braided jackets and crossed bandoleers as the man behind me and, if it had not been for the sil-

ver badges of office, one might well have been par-
doned for confusing them with those on the wrong
side of the law.

There was a strange uniformity in their general appearance. Heavy moustaches, unshaven chins, brood-
ing suspicious eyes. The only one not wearing his sombrero seemed to be in charge. "What have we here?"

"I'm delivering supplies by truck to Gomez of
Huila." I produced the *jefe's* travel permit and offered it to him. "My papers."

He examined it, then passed it back. "Luis Delgado,
at your orders, señor."

"At yours," I gave him politely.

"You intend to stay here tonight?"

"If it can be arranged."

"No difficulty, eh, Tacho?" He looked over his
shoulder at the old, white-haired man standing behind the small bar. "The señor desires accommodation. You will see to it?"

The old man, who was looking distinctly worried,
nodded eagerly and Delgado chuckled. "They jump,
these back-country pigs, when I crack the whip. You
will drink with me, señor?"

It seemed a reasonably politic thing to do. I downed
the glass of tequila he offered, gave him his health
and moved to the bar. The old man, Tacho, was
frightened—really frightened. There was a mute appeal in his eyes that I was unable to answer because I
didn't know what it was all about, not realising
then that these visits by Delgado and his men were an
old story.

Delgado slapped his hand hard down on the table.
"The food, you miserable worm. You turd. What
about our food?"

Tacho moved to the other end of the bar and the

door opened and a young woman came out of the kitchen. As I later discovered, she was barely past her seventeenth birthday, but looked a little older as women of mixed blood tend to do. She wore the usual ankle-length skirt, an Indian-work blouse and black hair hung down her back in a single braid.

She was small for I would say I had at least three inches on her and I can barely touch five and a half feet. Dark, dark eyes, high cheekbones, a wide mouth and a skin of palest olive that reminded me of my own mother, God rest her soul. She was not beautiful, yet after turning away I felt a compulsion to look at her again. Now why should that be?

Her face showed no emotion of any kind. She put the tray down on the table, turned to go and Delgado caught her wrist. "Heh, not so fast, little flower. An appetiser before the main course is the sensible man's way of eating."

He grabbed at the neck of the loose blouse, pulled it down and was put out to discover she was wearing a bodice underneath.

He roared with laughter. "Playing the lady, eh? We'll soon fix that."

She put her nails down his cheek, drawing blood and he slapped her solidly across the face as he might have slapped a man, forced her back across his knee as he put a hand up her skirt.

His friends were roaring with delight and, when old Tacho ran round the end of the bar and tried to intervene, someone sent him staggering back against the wall so forcibly that he fell to the ground.

The girl struggled desperately and two of the others got a wrist each and pinned her back across the table. She didn't scream, didn't show any fear at all, simply fought with all her strength, would struggle for her soul's sake to the final, bitter end, expecting nothing, not even from me, for when our eyes met, she looked through me as if I did not exist.

It was happening all over the country seven days a week, but that didn't make it any easier to swallow. No business of mine, so I pulled out the Enfield and blew the tequila bottle on the table into several score pieces.

The effect was considerable and I have seldom seen a group of men scatter so rapidly. Delgado was the only one who didn't move. He glanced back at me, still clutching the girl, his eyes wary, watchful, no fear there at all.

"Be easy, señor," he said softly. "Your turn will come."

"The next one is through the back of the skull," I told him. "Now move to the bar, hands high, all of you."

They obeyed reluctantly, warily, going backwards slowly, waiting their opportunity. The girl's reaction was interesting. She moved to my side and stood very close, holding on to my jacket tightly like a child recognising a loved one in a crowd after being lost.

Tacho had picked himself up from the floor and stood staring at me, shaken and dazed. I said, "Get their guns, old man, one-by-one. No need to fear. If anyone moves I'll shoot Delgado through the belly."

He didn't seem to hear me. Simply stood there swaying from side-to-side. I spoke to the girl without looking at her. "What's your name?"

There was no reply, but her grip tightened on my jacket. Delgado laughed harshly. "No help there, my friend. Little flower hasn't had a word to say for herself in years."

I reached down for the hand that clutched at my

jacket and brought her round to the front where I could see her face which was calm and watchful.

"You understand me?" She nodded. "Right, get their guns and don't be afraid. I will kill any man who tries to harm you."

Something stirred deep down in those dark eyes, something happened to her face, although it was difficult to say what exactly. In any event, she turned and moved towards the men at the bar.

A spur jangled in the stillness behind me. I started to turn, remembering too late that there had been six horses at the hitching rail, which meant another *rurale* not present in the room, and was struck a heavy blow somewhere behind the right ear which put me down on my hands and knees before I knew where I was.

The Enfield fired when it hit the floor, for as I have said elsewhere, all that delicate trigger mechanism needed was a touch. There was noise, confusion, a dull pain in the chest where a boot landed. I didn't really lose consciousness and finally surfaced to find myself on my knees, hands tied behind my back.

Delgado was busy fashioning a noose at the end of a length of saddle rope. He patted my face gently, then slipped the noose over my head and tossed the other end across a beam.

Two of his men held the struggling girl, the other three got on the rope behind me. Delgado smiled. "At first we hang you only a trifle. Then we have some fun with little flower. You should enjoy that. Afterwards—we'll see. I'll try to think of something special. A fine gentleman like you deserves it."

The rope tightened under my chin, jerking back my head, pulling me upright to sway on tip-toes before him. Old Tacho crouched in a chair by the wall, a hand to his mouth, eyes round, even the girl stopped struggling and her captors slackened their grip, watching me. Waiting.

The door opened and Father van Horne stepped into the room, lowering his head to get through. "Good evening," he said harshly.

He was holding a Gladstone bag in his right hand and presented a strangely menacing picture in his shabby, dust-covered cassock, the shovel hat shading the great, bearded face, another of those cigarillos jutting from his teeth.

"You would appear to have got yourself into a little trouble, Mr. Keogh," he observed.

The men holding the other end of the rope had slackened their grip in astonishment and I managed to breathe again.

"Let's say I got bored with standing by doing nothing, Father," I told him.

Delgado had his pistol out in a second, reached for the girl and pulled her out of the way.

"Who are you?" he demanded. "We weren't expecting any priest in these parts. I would have known."

"So I observe," van Horne said. "Would there be any point in asking you to release this man?"

Delgado smiled nastily. "You could always try, but that might make me angry. I might remember that I haven't hung a priest lately and the temptation to string you up beside this other gringo might well prove irresistible."

"That would be most unfortunate," van Horne said.

"For you, not for me. Now let's see your papers and quick about it."

"Happy to accommodate you, señor." Van Horne put the Gladstone bag down on the table and produced a key. "Humiliation, Mr. Keogh, is a specific for many ailments. It does a man good to get down on his belly occasionally and repent, if you follow me."

I didn't. Not until he opened the Gladstone bag, took out a Thompson sub-machine gun and blew the top of Delgado's head off.

THREE

It was all over very quickly. The men who had
been waiting to haul me over the beam let go the rope
and reached for their pistols. They were too late. As I
flung myself forward, my shoulder catching the girl behind the knees, bringing her down with me, van
Horne took care of all three, the stream of heavy bullets knocking them back against the wall.

He certainly knew his business. There was a round
drum magazine on the Thompson and he kept firing,
swinging in a wide arc which shattered the mirror behind the bar and ripped up the floor behind the two
remaining *rurales* who were running for the kitchen
door.

The first one made it, mainly because his companion acted as a shield, the bullets driving him headfirst
through the door, shredding the brocade jacket across
his back, the material bursting into flames.

The rear door banged as the lone survivor ran into the darkness and van Horne went after him.

The girl rolled over and sat up. I got to my knees
with some difficulty because of my bound hands. "Are
you all right?" I asked her.

She nodded, turned Delgado over, pulled a knife
from his belt and sliced through my bonds. When I
got the noose from around my neck the skin was raw

and broken on one side. The girl examined it, her face still quite expressionless, then got to her feet and ran into the kitchen.

Outside, a horse broke into a sudden gallop, there was a wild cry followed by the sound of another burst from the Tommy gun. I got to my feet and looked around me. There was blood everywhere, the stench of cordite and burning flesh, a butcher's shop in hell. Tacho was behind the bar pouring tequila into a tumbler, his hand shaking.

I reached for the bottle and a glass and helped myself. It was the nearest thing to pure alcohol I have ever drunk, but it pulled the pieces together again, which was what I needed.

"Not so good is it?" I said.

Tacho's face had sagged into complete despair. "To kill the police, even the *rurales,* is a very bad thing and there's a lot of federal cavalry out between here and Huila. There has been much trouble in this area lately."

The girl appeared with a stone jar containing some kind of grease. She rubbed a little into the raw places on my neck, frowning slightly in concentration, her fingers delicate and birdlike, then tore a strip of muslin off her petticoat and wound it round my neck a couple of times.

I patted her face. "That's a lot better. I'm very grateful."

She smiled for the first time, glanced uncertainly at Tacho, then went back into the kitchen. "Your daughter?"

He shook his head. "Her name is Balbuena, señor. Victoria Balbuena. Her father owned a hacienda near here. I used to work for him. Five years ago it was burned to the ground during the fighting and the *patrón* and his wife perished. Victoria saw it all. She was twelve at the time, only a child. Something happened to her, something most strange."

"What do you mean?"

"Oh, up here in the head, señor." He tapped his skull. "She has been unable to speak from that day to this."

There was a step in the doorway and van Horne moved inside, the cigarillo still clamped between his teeth, the machine gun under his arm.

"What happened?" I demanded.

"He got away, that's what damn well happened."

It was as if a cloak had slipped away revealing another kind of man entirely underneath. Everything had changed, the way he moved and walked and his voice had become harsher, the speech clipped, incisive. There was a powerful, elemental force to the man which he had kept hidden before for obvious reasons.

He slammed the machine gun down on the bar and snapped his fingers at Tacho. "Give me a bottle quick. Anything. I've got to think this out."

My Enfield was stuck in Delgado's belt. I pulled it free, checked the loading mechanically and shoved it into its holster. I stirred Delgado's body with my toe. "Something else you picked up on the Western Front, Father?"

"Son," he said solemnly, placing a hand on my shoulder. "I've got a confession to make. All is not what it seems."

"It very seldom is."

He laughed, that strange, harsh laugh of his. "Explanations can wait till a more suitable time. Right now, I've got other fish to fry. This is a mess. How long before the guy who got away reaches friends?"

"Tacho says there are *federales* all over the place

between here and Huila. There's been a lot of trouble
in the area lately. Did you mean it when you said you
were hoping to get through the Sierras to Guayamas?"

"Yes, a friend of mine tells me they get trading
schooners in there all the time from the Pacific is-
lands with cargoes of copra. It seemed to me like a
nice quiet way to leave."

"And you need that kind of passage out?"

"I think you could say that. I'll go and get a map."

He went out to the Mercedes and while he was
gone, the girl Victoria, came in from the kitchen with
a pot of coffee on a tray and several cups. When she
filled them, she served me first which was, for some
reason, curiously disturbing. She stood at the end of
the bar watching me gravely, not even responding
when I smiled at her, like some good dog waiting for
its master's command. Van Horne came in briskly
with a large-scale map of northern Mexico which he
spread out across the bar counter.

"North, south or east seem out of the question to
me," he said. "They'll be telegraphing ahead of us
within a few hours."

"Which only leaves the Sierras." I ran my finger
along the road to Huila. "That way would be by far
the best. The road through the mountains branches
off about forty miles this side of Huila."

"We'd never get that far, not without running into
trouble."

"You're including me in this business?"

"Have you any choice? You'll swing anyway if they
ever lay hands on you, and two could make out better
than one if things get a little rough."

In other words he needed me. The true reason for
his suggestion as I realised a moment later when he
slammed a hand down hard on the map.

"God, what a mess. Why the hell couldn't I mind my own business?"

Which had already occurred to me, but I said nothing. It was Tacho who spoke then, leaning over the map, squinting at it short-sightedly. "There is another way through the mountains by way of the Nonava Pass. A very bad road and seldom used, but during the Revolution some Yankee gringos brought arms through from the coast that way in two trucks. It has never been done since to my knowledge."

"He could be on to something," van Horne said. "They'd never look for us going through that way if what he says is true."

"What about petrol?"

"There's still about twenty-five gallons in the tank including the reserve and I'm carrying another fifty in the boot in five-gallon cans. Enough to get us all the way to the coast."

I looked at the map again. We had to stay with the road to Huila for about fifteen miles, indeed had no choice in the matter. Then we cut off across the foothills through rough country, following what was obviously going to be little more than an old pack trail.

"We could run into trouble out there in the dark," I said. "Lights or no lights."

"So what do we do? Sit on our backsides till sunrise and the *federales* get here? Be your age, Keogh. Sure, we might end up nose down in a hole or even drive straight over the edge of some *arroyo*, but we don't exactly have a choice, do we, so let's get moving."

He folded his map, grabbed an unopened bottle of tequila and went out. I said to Tacho, "He's got a point. No sense in hanging about."

The girl caught me by the arm as I turned away.

Her eyes tried to speak for her, the mouth opened and shut, the whole face working.

"What is it?" I demanded.

"I think she wishes to go with you, señor," Tacho said.

She nodded eagerly as I turned to her and I took her by the shoulders and gave her a shake. "Don't be a damn fool. What could I do with you? Where would you go? I'm running for my life."

She gripped my hands convulsively, the eyes still pleading and I shook my head. "No, it just isn't on."

Something went out of her, I don't know quite what. Hope perhaps, or something even more important to her. Some vital essence that is in all of us. She turned away, her shoulders sagging.

Tacho said, "In a way, she is running too, señor. For such a young one, she has known much sadness, many bad things. The Balbuenas were a name in these parts, and her father was a great aristocrat, but he committed the unforgiveable sin for one of the high blood. He married an Indian. More than that—a Yaqui. A woman from the Wind River country. His family never forgave him."

"So the girl has no one?"

"Not here, señor, but on the other side of the mountains where her mother was born it would be a different story."

"All right," I said to the girl, bowing to the inevitable. "I'll give you two minutes to get your things together."

She gave me one startled glance over her shoulder, then disappeared into the kitchen. "Sometimes God looks down through the clouds, señor," Tacho said.

"Not very often in my experience. What about

you? How will the *federales* treat you?"

"An innocent bystander and roughly treated, señor." He shrugged. "Besides, where would I go, an old man like me?"

The Mercedes horn sounded impatiently and a moment later, Victoria came in from a kitchen, clutching a small bundle, a heavy woollen shawl about her shoulders.

"You will look after her, señor," Tacho called as I pushed her towards the door. "She is in your care from now on."

A disturbing thought to know that one had some sort of responsibility towards another human being again, but too late to draw back now.

As we approached the Mercedes I took the girl's bundle and threw it into the back. Van Horne said, "What in the hell do you think you're playing at?"

"The girl goes with us," I said. "No arguments."

"Over my dead body."

"That could be arranged," I told him flatly.

I didn't know what would happen next, already had a hand to the butt of the Enfield in the darkness, when surprisingly be capitulated.

"Oh, get her inside for God's sake and let's get out of here. I can always crack your skull later."

I put her into the rear seat, climbed in next to him and he drove away.

The fifteen miles for which we stayed with the Huila road were no problem and took us about thirty minutes to cover, a remarkable performance considering the darkness and the state of the road.

It was when we reached the place where we were to turn off that we ran into difficulties. For one thing it took a good half-hour to find the start of the trail, so faintly was it marked. When we turned onto it, I knew we were in trouble.

It was almost impossible to see, even with the headlamps full on and we seemed to be threading our way through a ghostly maze of thorn bushes and organ cactus. We kept this up for a while, crawling at five or ten miles an hour for most of the time and on two occasions it was only van Horne's quick reflexes that prevented us from plunging into a dry arroyo.

In the end he braked to a halt, and switched off the engine and lights. "So you were right and I was wrong. I don't even know if we're on the trail any more. We'll move on at first light."

I turned and looked back at the girl. "Are you all right?"

She reached for my hand, pressed it gently. Van Horne said, "Now may I ask why in the hell you had to bring her along? Can't you do without it or something?"

"The *federales* would have passed her from hand-to-hand."

"If it doesn't happen to her here, it happens somewhere else," he said. "So what's the point?"

"Her mother's people live on the other side of the mountains. They'll take her in. Look after her properly. Yaquis have a strong kinship system. They wouldn't turn her away."

He was in the act of lighting one of his cigarillos and turned to look at me in surprise, the match flaring in his cupped hands. "Are you saying she's Yaqui?"

"Her mother was. Her father was straight out of the top drawer. One of the big land-owning families."

"Son, that doesn't mean a damn thing. She's

branded clean to the bone. Why the Yaquis are worse than the Apache and that's going some, believe me. First night she doesn't like you in bed, she'll take a knife to your privates."

"My affair, not yours."

"It touches both of us while we're together. You get rid of her the moment we break through to the other side, understand?"

"We'll see about that."

"We certainly will." And then, with one of those puzzling about-turns that I was to find so typical of the man, added, "It's going to get a damn sight colder than this before morning. If she cares to lift up the back seat she'll find some car rugs."

He turned, as if suddenly exasperated and repeated the information in Spanish. The girl stood up and fumbled about in the darkness. After a while, she passed a heavy car rug over to me.

"No, for you," I said.

Van Horne laughed uneasily. "She's going to hang onto you like a leech, Keogh. You mark my words." He grabbed an end of the rug, unfolded it and spread it across our knees. "She should be snug enough back there. There are two more. On the other hand I don't mind if you want to get under the covers with her."

I think he was deliberately trying to bait me. I refused to be drawn, but turned and said to the girl, "Wrap up well and go to sleep. We'll move on at first light."

Van Horne switched on the dashboard light, found the bottle of tequila he had taken from the bar and uncorked it.

He took a long pull and sighed. "Heaven alone knows what this stuff does to the liver, but it's all that's going to get me through this night. You'd better have some."

I took a mouthful, fought for breath as it burned its way down and handed the bottle back hurriedly. "I think old Tacho must have made that himself in the back room."

"I can believe that all right. I can believe anything of this damned country." He shivered. "God, if I had my time over again."

"Would anything be any different?"

The neck of the bottle chinked on his teeth, there was a gurgle, a long gurgle and then he sighed. "No, it's a long, dark night at the mouth of nowhere, Keogh, and we're both far from home, so the truth for once."

"Which is . . . ?"

"The old, old question." He laughed shortly. "Would you believe me, Keogh, if I told you I spent four years in a seminary? That I actually trained for the priesthood?"

"You certainly made a convincing enough job of it at Huerta this morning when they were executing those men."

It was as if I had touched an open wound and he turned on me sharply. "They were dying, Keogh, they'd only minutes to live. They went easier thinking they'd had a priest. Whether they did or not doesn't matter a damn where they are now."

"So you think they've gone to a happier place, do you?"

It was a stupid and ill-judged remark in the circumstances and received the reply it merited. "Don't get clever with me, boy."

"All right, I'm sorry." He took another pull at the

bottle and passed it to me. "What do you do when you're not wearing a cassock?"

"You might say I'm in the banking business." He laughed loudly and without the slightest sign of having drink taken in spite of the quantity he'd already put away. "Yes, I like that. You know I was once in a little town in Arkansas where the local police insisted on a permit if you owned a hand gun and you had to state your reason for needing one."

"What did you put?"

"I told them I often carried large sums of money. I didn't say it was usually other people's."

"I see—so you're a thief."

"I rob banks, if that's what you mean and believe me you've got to be good to get away with it."

"Which is why you're running round Mexico playing the earnest priest?"

"That's it exactly. I knocked over the National Bank at a little place called Brownsville in Texas two days ago all on my own. It's a funny thing, but priests and nuns—everybody trusts them. I knocked on that door a half-hour before time and the guard opened it without a qualm."

"How many dead men did you leave behind you?"

"Dead men." He seemed surprised. "I told you it was a nice, clean job. Four guys lying on their faces with their hands tied and an empty vault was all I left behind that day." He leaned forward as if trying to see my face. "Anyway, how many men have you killed, Keogh, that's the question."

He was right, but if I'd told him, I'd have given him the shock of his life. "One too many."

"It always is, even when you think you've got an ex-

cuse for it like you with your politics. We're a
lot alike you and me, Keogh, in our different ways and
I'll tell you why. We've both got death in the soul, it's
as simple as that."

Which was probably the most terrible thing anyone had ever said to me, mainly because it was the
kind of remark that brings out into the open a truth
one has always attempted to avoid.

"What was it you called it?" van Horne said. "The
last place God made. That about sums it up. My old
lady would say I'd ended up with what I deserved.
She and my father were Pennsylvania Dutch. Moved
to Vermont when he opened a little printing shop in
Altoona. Her religion was everything to her. Believe
me, boy, nobody takes it more seriously than Dutch
Catholics. When I walked out of that seminary on account of a stupid, little bitch who left me six months
later, my mother laid it straight on the line. The
Wrath of God and the Day of Judgement rolled into
one. That's what I'm going to get and any time now
the way things are going."

He rambled on in this way for quite some time, not
drunk and yet it was the drink talking. Finally, it
started to rain in great, heavy cold drops that hurt
where they made contact. We got out quickly and put
the top up and only just in time for the rain soon increased into a persistent downpour.

"My God, this is all we needed," van Horne said.

I wondered if he appreciated the seriousness of this
new turn of events. That by morning, half the
ground we had to traverse would be quagmire and a
hundred dry arroyos, rushing torrents and quite im-
passable.

There seemed little point in going into that now
and it certainly wouldn't change anything so I

pulled an end of the car rug around my legs against the cold and turned up my collar.

How many men have you killed, Keogh? It was a hell of a thought to go to sleep on.

The morning dawned grey and bleak, heavy rain still falling. We had stopped close to the edge of what had once been a dry stream bed. Water was rushing through it now in full spate like a moorland burn on a November morning back home. The mountains were closer than I had expected and we got out the map and finally managed to place ourselves.

We had about ten or twelve miles of open country to traverse before reaching the trail we were seeking, the one which would take us up through the Nonava Pass. It was marked quite clearly on the map between two mountains, one a sugar-loaf and the other with three distinctively jagged peaks. We could see them both in the distance quite clearly in spite of the rain.

That magnificent engine fired without difficulty when van Horne pressed the self-starter and he took the Mercedes away slowly, working out his route as he went, for any remaining trace of the track we had been following had been washed out by the heavy rain.

It was still bitterly cold and the girl, Victoria, stayed muffled in the two car rugs she had used during the night and peered out into the morning, her face as serious and grave as ever. I asked her if she was all right and she nodded and actually smiled, which was something.

Van Horne said, "How come you speak Spanish as well as you do?"

"My mother was born in Seville."

"Is that so? Your old man must have got around. I picked mine up in Juárez one year, working as manager in a small casino there. I had to stay out of circulation for a while on account of the fact that I'd broken out of Leavenworth—that's the Texas State Penitentiary."

"What were you in there for?"

"Shooting a guy who was trying to shoot me, only he had friends at court and I didn't."

Strange, the change in him. The brash, confident manner, the excessive toughness in the voice as if he was trying to prove something, though whether to me or himself was debatable. I was thinking about that for want of something better to do when we went over a slight rise a couple of minutes later and saw federal cavalry in the hollow below.

They were saddled up and grouped in a rough circle as if waiting to receive their orders after breaking camp. The surprise was mutual and the whisper of the engine at the slow speed at which we were moving combined with the heavy rain, explained why they had not heard our approach.

There was a single, excited cry as we were seen and as van Horne swung the wheel and slammed his foot hard down, a couple of shots whistled through the air. We went down the slope in a great sliding loop that took us through a patch of water a foot deep and out into the final stretch of open plain rising into the mountains.

By now, the hunt was up with a vengeance and the result by no means a foregone conclusion for the *federales*, as usual, were superbly mounted and try as he could, there were stretches where van Horne had no option but to slow down considerably.

We were perhaps two hundred yards in the lead

when he cursed and braked sharply as we went over a small ridge and found the way blocked by a flooded arroyo. By the time we had extricated ourselves, the gap had narrowed to no more than fifty yards. We started to climb steeply, cutting across a broad shoulder at the foot of the sugar-loaf mountain, the wheels spinning in the loose shale.

"Once over the top there we're certain to hit that trail," he shouted. "They don't stand a cat in hell's chance of keeping up with us. The Thompson's under your feet. Give them a little discouragement."

I pulled out the celebrated Gladstone bag and found the sub-machine gun inside resting on top of dozens of packets of crisp bank notes. An interesting discovery, but I had more important things on my mind. I leaned out and loosed off a long, rolling burst well above the heads of our pursuers. It certainly started them reining in, but when I attempted to repeat the performance, the drum magazine jammed, a common fault with them at that time.

The *federales* urged their mounts up the slope, but a moment later, we were over the shoulder of the hill and saw the trail quite plainly no more than fifty yards below us. It was in much better condition than I had expected and the moment we reached it and the Mercedes started to climb, I knew we were home and dry.

Van Horne turned and grinned savagely at me, dropping a gear as the trail lifted along the side of the ravine and then, as he looked back, he gave a sudden exclamation and jammed on the brakes. A whole slice of mountain seemed to have broken away in a great wave of earth and rock, probably a result of the heavy rain during the night, wiping the trail off the map for all time.

He slammed the gear stick into reverse, and started to turn the Mercedes, but he was already too late as a dozen or so *federales* came over the rise and boiled around us like an angry sea.

The Enfield was ready in my hand and there was little doubt that I could have dropped a couple of them, but no more than that, which seemed rather futile in the circumstances. I put it down on the seat and raised my hands as ostentatiously as I could.

FOUR

The next few minutes could well have been my last and probably almost were. I got a boot between the shoulder blades as I stepped out of the Mercedes that put me down on my hands and knees. No place to be with a dozen horses doing their best to trample me into the ground. I was kicked twice, the second time with such force that I thought a rib had gone and then a grip of iron fastened on my collar and brought me to my feet.

Van Horne steadied me with one hand and swung a fist into the rump of the nearest horse with such force that it reared up, almost unseating its rider. Someone struck at him with a plaited leather riding whip. He allowed it to curl around his arm, then pulled the owner from the saddle with no apparent effort, the first hint I'd been given of the man's enormous strength.

There was considerable confusion for a moment or two after that as the soldiers frantically hauled their mounts out of the way to avoid trampling their unfortunate companion. One or two of them drew sabres and for a moment things looked decidedly nasty and then a single pistol shot sounded and a young officer burst through the outer ring and reined in sharply.

He had a thin, sallow face, a dark smudge of moustache and wore the silver bars of a lieutenant. Unlike most of his men, he was not wearing a rubber poncho and his tailored uniform was soaked with rain.

He smiled coldly, leaned down from the saddle and touched van Horne between the eyes with the barrel of the pistol. "Large or small, strong or weak, señor, one bullet is all it takes."

"Just call the dogs off, that's all," van Horne told him. "We'll come quietly."

"You will indeed. My orders were to apprehend you alive if possible, but I would be happy for you to give me an excuse to act otherwise. I find you an affront to all decency. Take off that cassock."

Van Horne glared at him, hands on hips. "And what if I tell you to go and do the other thing, you pip-squeak."

The lieutenant dismounted, tossed the reins of his horse to one of his men and faced van Horne squarely, raising his revolver to belt level. He thumbed back the hammer very deliberately.

"Señor, for reasons of my own, which are none of your business, I do not like you or anything about you. I assure you now, on my mother's grave, that if you do not do exactly as I say, I will give you what you so richly deserve."

He was no longer smiling and if one looked closely, the gun was shaking a little. Van Horne raised a hand as if to placate him. "All right, soldier boy, anything for a quiet life."

He unbuttoned his cassock at the neck, pulled it over his head and tossed it into the Mercedes. He was wearing a pair of very clerical-looking trousers in black worsted and a white shirt.

The lieutenant said, "The collar also, if you please."

Van Horne removed it and threw it into the Mercedes after the cassock. "Satisfied?" he demanded.

"Only when I see you hang, señor," the lieutenant said. "You will now drive this automobile back down the trail under my instructions. The slightest attempt to escape and I shoot. You understand me?"

"You've got a big mouth with that in your hand, that's all I understand, sonny." Van Horne turned and moved back to the Mercedes.

"You can walk," the lieutenant told me and started after van Horne.

"What about her?" I nodded towards the girl who was being held quite unnecessarily by two of his men. "Can't you take her with you?"

He looked towards her and frowned. "She's the one from old Tacho's place, isn't she? The one who can't speak."

"That's right. Have you spoken to him? Did he tell you what happened last night?"

"No, but I've had a reasonably full account from the sole survivor of the *rurales* you butchered."

"Very interesting," I said. "Did he tell you what they were trying to do with the girl? Did he mention they were about to hang me for trying to intervene? Would have finished me off if my friend there hadn't arrived when he did?"

He believed me, which was the only important thing, his face turning paler than ever and the expression on his eyes was terrible to see.

"A dirty world, Lieutenant," I said softly. "And that kid couldn't even raise a scream to save herself."

He turned away without a word, grabbed Victoria by the arm and shoved her into the back seat of the Mercedes, then climbed in beside van Horne and told him to get moving. It took van Horne quite a bit of manoeuvring to get the Mercedes pointing the right way but he managed it after a while and we all got out of the way to let him drive past.

We started down the trail, the rest of us, the troopers riding, but the sergeant in charge, a small dark-haired man with a heavy moustache, dismounted and walked beside me, a pistol in his hand.

I produced a packet of Artistas. "All right if I smoke?"

"Sure, I'll have one with you." I gave him a light and he blew out the first lungful of smoke expertly. "Had yourselves a ball last night at old Tacho's, you and your pal, didn't you? How many *rurales* was it you saw off—five?"

"What's happening now?'" I asked.

"Oh, the colonel's waiting to see you down there. Colonel Bonilla. He's the military governor in this region. He joined us for a routine patrol yesterday morning, just to see how things were going for himself. He's like that. We were bivouacked for the night at an old *rancheria* near the main road when this *rurale* rode up. The one you let slip through your fingers at Tacho's." There was sincere admiration in his voice when he added, "'You and your pal must be hell on wheels."

"What made you come straight out here instead of going to Tacho's?"

"That was the colonel." He put a finger to his nose. "He's really got it upstairs, that one. He figured you'd make a break for it so he only sent half-a-dozen guys to Tacho's with a sergeant in charge, then he had a look at the map with the lieutenant. He said if it was him, he'd make a break for it through the Nonava Pass because it didn't look possible."

"He certainly hit the nail right on the head."

"He usually does. He pushed us hard last night. Only stopped when it really started to rain, but he was right again. If we hadn't been where we were, you'd have got through, wouldn't you?"

Quite a man, this Colonel Bonilla. We reached the place where the trail finally merged with the desert to find the Mercedes standing in the entrance to a narrow ravine. Someone had already started a fire in spite of the rain, no great feat with so many thorn bushes around and the smoke curled lazily on the damp air.

Van Horne was standing beside the Mercedes and I realised that someone, presumably Bonilla, was sitting in the rear seat, the door open. He was a tall, handsome man with sideburns which were prematurely white for I judged him to be no more than forty years of age. He made a rather gallant figure in his caped cavalry greatcoat and he had an intelligent, cynical air to him, the face of a man who has seen it all, everything possible in life and simply doesn't believe in anything any more.

The sergeant handed me over to the lieutenant who took me the rest of the way. Bonilla looked me over calmly.

"Your name, señor," he asked politely.

"Emmet Keogh. I'm a British citizen."

"Keogh?" He frowned slightly. "An unusual name, señor, and I have heard it before. You are the one who was in charge of security at the silver mines at Hermosa."

"That's right. You seem surprised."

"You are not what I would have looked for, señor. I had expected a different kind of man."

"In what way? Two horns and a tail?"

"Possibly even that. Your papers."

I took out the travel permit signed by the *jefe* in Bonito. "That's all I've got with me."

He examined it gravely. "So, you are supposed to be delivering a truck-load of supplies to this man Gomez in Huila."

"That's right. For Señor Janos, the owner of the Hotel Blanco in Bonito."

"To know Señor Janos is not much of a recommendation, believe me. This man has just given me his personal version of what happened at the way-station last night. Now I will hear yours." He nodded to the young lieutenant. "Take him away."

The lieutenant gave van Horne a shove to get started and none too gently. Bonilla chuckled. "I'm afraid Lieutenant Cordona doesn't care for your friend overmuch. You see he is a very correct young man. When he was a boy his parents intended him for the priesthood and he was educated to that end. You will readily understand that to someone like him, a man like your friend who represents himself to be a priest when he is not . . ."

He produced a silver cigarette case, selected one, lit it and blew smoke into the rain. "So, we will now hear what you have to say."

I told him the exact truth. When I had finished, he nodded slowly. "Remarkable—truly remarkable." He reached behind him and produced the Gladstone bag. "There are fifty-three thousand dollars in here, did you know that?"

"I saw van Horne for the first time yesterday morning in Bonito when he administered the last rites to three men who were publicly executed at the police barracks. He looked like a priest. He acted like a priest and that's what everyone took him to be, including me. When he walked in on what was happening at Tacho's last night, he saved me from getting my neck stretched. Saved the girl from God knows what . . . That should count for something, whatever else he may do."

"Whatever the circumstances, five at one blow, my friend, is a little hard to take, but we will speak again later when I've heard from my other patrol."

He snapped a finger and the sergeant moved in fast. "Put him with his friend and then get me some breakfast."

I joined van Horne who squatted against a rock. His shirt was plastered to his body and he was shivering slightly. "Well, what did you tell him?" he demanded.

"The truth—what else?"

"Fair enough." He smiled faintly. "Not that it will make any kind of difference. Only one way out of this, Keogh."

"Perhaps." I looked around me. "What happened to the girl?"

"They've put her to work."

She was wearing one of the cavalrymen's rubber ponchos and a military cap, which was why I hadn't noticed her at first, and she crouched beside the fire cooking *frijoles* in a frying pan.

She saw me looking, poured coffee into a mug and started toward us. Cordona beat her to it, knocked the mug from her hand and sent her back to her place at the fire with a shove.

"Now there's a guy I could really learn to hate," van Horne commented.

"The feeling's mutual. It seems he has a thing about people who pretend to be priests."

"I'm breaking my heart," van Horne said and

faintly in the distance, a cavalry trumpet sounded.

Half-a-dozen soldiers, a sergeant in the lead, rode out of the rain. "These will be the boys he sent on to Tacho's last night," I told van Horne.

We watched the sergeant go forward to make his report. Bonilla glanced towards us a couple of times, then appeared to question the man closely. Finally he called to Cordona to bring us to him.

"Tell me, Señor Keogh," he said. "What were you carrying in that truck of yours."

"Whisky," I said. "For delivery to a man called Gomez in Huila. I've already told you."

"But forgot to mention the rifles."

"Rifles?" I stared at him stupidly. "I don't know what you mean."

"Martini-Henry carbines. Those packing cases in the back of your truck are full of them, or so my sergeant here informs me and he's usually reliable."

"Nice friends you've got, Keogh," van Horne said bitterly. "I'd say that just about puts the lid on things."

"Why in the hell should it," I demanded angrily. "It's Janos who owns that truck, not me. He only hired me to drive the damned thing." I turned to Bonilla. "You've seen that permit for yourself. It's Janos you want. Janos and the *jefe* in Bonito, Captain Ortiz."

"All will be taken care of, Mr. Keogh, in God's good time." He ran a hand over the back of the Mercedes' driving seat. "This is really a very handsome vehicle." He turned to Cordona. "Did you know that I could drive an automobile, lieutenant? A minor accomplishment, but rewarding when presented with a machine like this. In fact I have decided to give myself the pleasure of driving back to Huila in it. Detail two men to accompany me. I should like to get started as soon as possible."

"And the prisoners, Colonel?"

"Oh, they can walk, I think. The exercise will prove both salutary and beneficial. You should arrive tomorrow afternoon. Report to me when you do."

He turned away, dismissing us completely and Cordona ordered us back to our original position. We watched the preparation for Bonilla's departure. Two soldiers clutching their carbines got in the rear seat and when Bonilla pressed the self-starter, the Mercedes rumbled into life for him as easily as it had for van Horne.

We watched him drive away into the rain and I said to van Horne, "Well, what do you think?"

"Think? What in the hell am I supposed to think." He glared angrily at me. "Be your age, Keogh. You've reached the end of the road and you'd better get used to the idea."

When we broke camp and moved out, the girl was put up on the back of one of the pack mules, Cordona's orders, but van Horne and I walked each at the end of thirty feet of rope, wrists lashed together.

I say walked, but in fact this meant keeping up with the horses come what may. When they trotted, we trotted too and when they cantered, we ran.

It was a hell of a morning for even after the rain stopped, the going was very rough and, on occasion, both of us fell to be dragged impatiently several yards.

We stopped at noon and again, a small fire was lit so that coffee could be heated. Van Horne and I crouched wearily on the ground beside the horses and watched. Everyone had coffee except us. The girl was particularly distressed by this. She glanced towards us constantly and once, filled a mug with coffee and pulled at Cordona's sleeve, but he shook his head impatiently.

"That creep has decided to make us suffer, do you know that?" van Horne said.

I'm beginning to think it the general idea. If only you'd played at being a Methodist. Maybe he wouldn't have minded so much."

For some reason that struck him as being really funny and he laughed out loud, which didn't please Cordona. He glared across angrily, then ordered his men to strike camp.

The afternoon was a repetition of the morning, which is to say it was another long agony that seemed as if it would never end. Towards evening, it started to rain heavily again and I stumbled along at the rear of the column, cold, wet and utterly wretched, my legs so tired that it was a small miracle each time I took another step.

When we finally made camp in the ruins of an old *ranchería* in the late evening, I collapsed on the ground and crawled into the shelter of a broken adobe wall the moment the trooper who had been leading me released the rope.

We had covered something like thirty miles and there were another twenty to go. I opened my eyes wearily and found van Horne beside me.

"I'm getting old, Keogh, that's what it is." His face looked grey and drawn and yet he still managed to smile. "You want to know something? I've decided I don't like our friend one little bit."

Three separate fires were lit, the men scavenging for wood in a nearby thicket and soon I could smell coffee and bacon on the damp air.

After a while, the girl appeared holding a tin mug of coffee in one hand, a pan containing a couple of frijoles in the other. Cordona arrived on the run and kicked the mug from her hand, catching her wrist and really hurting her.

"I said no food for these two, damn you," he said and then hesitated, obviously considerably put out at the sight of the pain in her face.

"Does that make you feel better, sonny?" van Horne asked him.

Cordona turned, a fist raised, restraining himself only with the greatest difficulty, then grabbed the girl by the arm and pushed her back towards the fire.

The rain increased and so did our misery as darkness fell. Several of the troopers glanced towards us as we crouched there in the heavy rain. Cordona ignored us. Simply sat at his own small fire chain-smoking and drinking cup after cup of coffee.

Finally the girl, Victoria, got up very deliberately, picked up two horse blankets and came towards us. She gave one to van Horne, then crouched beside me and spread the other one around both of us. Men glanced furtively at Cordona, then at each other. I could hear the whispering and yet he made no sign, staring straight ahead of him, too proud to provoke an incident.

I was shaking like a leaf, my teeth chattering, but already I was beginning to warm up, the girl's body pressed against me. When the shaking continued, she pulled my face down into her shoulders and drew the blanket over my head, rocking gently to and fro. I forgot her age then, forgot her background as my eyes started to close in sleep. She was just a woman doing the right thing at the right time and all women, after all, are born old and knowing most things.

It stopped raining during the night and the following day dawned to a sky of cloudless blue, the sun starting his climb early. By mid-morning it was so hot that all moisture had been sucked out of that barren land again and dust rose in a great cloud stirred by the horses' hooves.

Van Horne and I marched in the thick of it, which didn't make breathing any easier and the heat was unbearable. By the time we were ready for the noonday halt, I was at the end of my tether and beyond. I had fallen so many times that the column had to be halted constantly and even Cordona had raised no objection when I was given water.

I'd existed in my own small world of suffering and had been unaware of how van Horne was managing. When I finally opened my eyes and found him lying beside me at the noonday camp, he seemed in no better case than I was myself.

"I've decided to live, just to spite this guy," he croaked faintly. "A small victory, but mine own."

I rolled over on my back, my whole body on fire, and found Victoria kneeling over me with a canteen of water. She looked frightened and yet angry at the same time. I tried a smile, but my lips were cracking and it hurt.

She poured a little water into my mouth, then bathed my face. Cordona walked across from the fire, a mug of coffee in one hand and stood looking down at us.

"Satisfied?" van Horne croaked. "Or were we supposed to die?"

Cordona turned away and went back to the fire. Yet

he still wouldn't give in. When we resumed the journey, I was carried to one of the mules and my wrists looped over the high wooden pommel of a pack saddle. It meant that I couldn't fall down any more, which was something, but I still had to walk.

Van Horne was undergoing the same treatment a few yards in front of me and this was the manner in which we covered the final miles into Huila, although in my case it was simply a matter of hanging on, for my toes seemed to be trailing most of the time.

I have no clear memory of entering Huila itself, only of surfacing to a bucket of water in the face and finding myself on my back, Cordona leaning over me.

"All right, Keogh, pull yourself together," he said. "You're here."

A couple of soldiers dragged me to my feet and we started across the courtyard. Van Horne was ahead of me, also supported by two soldiers and we went through a large oaken door to a smell that said I was back in prison again.

The cell was no better than a sewer which was, I suppose, the intention. Even that wasn't enough for Cordona and he had them place us in leg irons before leaving. I was past caring and as the door clanged shut, plunged into blissful, easeful dark.

I must have slept for sixteen or seventeen hours after that. I can remember waking a couple of times to relieve myself and finding van Horne snoring in the corner and on each occasion, plunged into a deep sleep again by the simple expedient of closing my eyes.

When I finally awakened, it was late afternoon of the following day and van Horne was standing by the small, barred window of the cell looking out.

He turned with a smile. "How do you feel?"

"Terrible." I put a hand to my belly, which felt as if there was a hole in it. "Is there anything to eat around here?"

"You'll find a pan of slops in the corner with so many maggots in it I lost count. I'm waiting for your girl friend."

"Victoria." I got up and groaned involuntarily at the stiffness in my limbs. "What are you talking about?"

"She was here at the window earlier so I slipped her a fifty peso note I had in my shoe to go and get us a few things." He grunted suddenly. "Here she comes now."

I peered through the bars into a small courtyard with a fountain in the centre. There didn't seem to be anyone about and the gate to the street outside stood open.

Victoria looked up at me, her face grave and anxious. I said softly, "You shouldn't be doing this."

She smiled and started to pass things through the bars one-by-one. A bottle of wine, bread, olives, a couple of long sausages and two packets of Artistas and matches.

"Good appetite, my friends." Colonel Bonilla stepped out of the shadows of an archway to the right of us.

"Don't take it out on the girl, Bonilla," I said as he approached. "She was only trying to help."

She looked up at him anxiously. He patted her on the head and said, "On your way, child, and stay out of trouble."

To my amazement, she smiled for him, fleetingly and yet it was there, and smiled again for me before hurrying away.

Bonilla said, "Yes, my friends, it is always wise to eat well when you can, for in this life, one can never be certain if one will ever be able to eat again."

On which pleasant note he left us to eat and disappeared into the shadows of the archway.

FIVE

My father, a dedicated Fenian till the day he died of tuberculosis in an English prison, left me to the care of my grandfather, Mickeen Bawn Keogh of Stradballa in the county of Kerry.

Now it must be understood that Mickeen Bawn means small white Michael, a description that never made much sense to me, for although his hair had been snow white since boyhood, he was six and a half feet tall. A gentle giant of a man except with the drink taken. In that state, I have seen half-a-dozen hard men of their hands run from him, for in his youth he had been, amongst other things, a prize-fighter.

So, I was raised on a Kerry farm along with the best horses in Ireland, which is to say the world, and nothing else life has to offer could ever match up to those days. Back country so quiet you could hear a dog barking in the next county. Sweet-smelling mornings and sunsets to thank God for. No beginning, no end, time a circle until the day my grandfather decided I had brains and sent me to the Jesuits at Knockbree to be made into a scholar and perhaps even a gentleman.

When I was accepted by the College of Surgeons, went up to the university, there was no prouder man and yet each of us is what he is from the day he is born and no escaping. I went to Dublin town to learn something of the art of healing and met a man called Michael Collins who found another use for me.

After the Easter Rising, I went back to the university on his orders and bided my time. Stayed there during the years that followed. A medical student by day, which was as good a front as you could find, and a member of the Squad in my spare time. Emmet Oge Keogh—little Edmund Keogh. His strong left hand, he used to call me and God knows, I killed for him often enough in those days or for Ireland, whichever way you care to look at it.

Some of these things I spoke of to van Horne during the first three days after our capture. The fact is I found that I rather liked the man because he reminded me pleasantly of my grandfather. In any case, there was little else to do except talk for we were given no work, no exercise of any description during those first few days.

We were even reduced to eating the slops provided once a day in an old enamel bucket at noon because there were no more visits from Victoria with supplies from the town. After that first evening when Bonilla had appeared, there was a guard posted outside the window.

Three days we had of it and that was three days too much with tempers starting to fray. I remember van Horne standing at the window, just before dark, trying to get a little air, suddenly turning in a kind of irritation, looking for someone to kick at.

"They tell me you never had more than ten thousand men under arms against the English at any one time. What was wrong with the rest of the country?"

He was trying to bait me for some reason of his own, I knew that, but I would not be drawn. "We didn't have the arms for more."

"Come off it, Keogh." He laughed harshly and wiped the sweat from his face with an old rag. "I think guys like you, the ones who turned out, did it because you got a bang out of killing people. You enjoyed it, the whole thing. A game for schoolboys playing with real guns."

"You could be right there," I said cheerfully, taking the last cigarette from my crumpled packet of Artistas.

He was annoyed and said sourly, "Didn't I read somewhere that there was so much shooting in the back going on they had to introduce a law making it compulsory for any man passing a policeman on the street to raise his hands in the air?"

"I believe that was so in some areas."

"I just bet it was." By now, he was thoroughly irritated. "How many did you see off then, Keogh, for the sake of your bloody cause?"

"Why, as many as was needed Mr. van Horne," I told him evenly.

He stood there staring at me, really angry like some great sullen bull getting ready to charge. What would have happened next is debatable, but the course of action was chosen for us as a key rattled in the lock.

Lieutenant Cordona entered, spic and span in a freshly pressed khaki drill uniform, highly polished boots glistening in the dim light.

"Well, damn me if it isn't the soldier," van Horne said. "Don't tell me we're going to get some service at last."

"You will get more than that, I assure you," Cordona replied and motioned us outside.

He took us out through the courtyard between half-a-dozen soldiers, leg irons rattling on the cobbles. We went through an archway into a cloistered patio and finally entered a small, enclosed garden. There was a fountain, a flame tree vivid with blossom and Bonilla taking his ease in a wicker chair on the terrace.

Like Cordona, he wore a well-tailored uniform and highly polished boots and looked very correct, very military. He told Cordona to bring us inside, got to his feet and led the way in through open french windows.

The room was sparsely furnished and was obviously used as his office. There was a desk and chair, various large-scale maps of the area on the wall, a narrow iron cot in one corner and not much else.

He sat down behind the desk and put a cigar in his mouth, which Cordona lit for him. He leaned back in his chair, looked at us both for a reasonably lengthy interval and then spoke.

"Yes, in many ways you couldn't be more complementary to each other. It is really quite remarkable. Two rogues together."

"Oh, I wouldn't say that," van Horne said.

"Wouldn't you, Father? You don't mind if I still call you that, do you?"

"You can call me what you damn well please," van Horne told him cheerfully.

"Which gives me something of a choice. Murderer? Yes, many times over. Thief?" Bonilla turned to me. "Would you believe me, Señor Keogh, if I told you he would cut the fingers off a dead man to get at his rings? Totally without scruple or pity. In at least two states in the U.S.A. he faces the death sentence."

"Peck's Bad Boy, that's me," van Horne said. "So what?"

"And in excellent company, Father, I assure you. I

have here a most interesting communication from
Mexico City from the representative of the Irish Free
State. This Emmet Keogh is a very dangerous man.
An Irish gunman, he was for several years a member
of what was known as the Squad. An organisation
used by the Irish patriotic leader, Michael Collins, as
chief weapon in the campaign of deliberate terrorism
he waged against the English. Señor Keogh has killed
so many men he has lost count."

"For what it's worth, I was a soldier of the Irish Republican Army," I said.

"How noble. Were you fighting for Ireland when
you were trouble-shooter for the Hermosa Mining
Company, señor? How many men did you kill in the
disturbances up there. Four or was it five?"

"They'd hung a priest as you damn well know," I
told him. "I was doing what I was paid for."

He ignored me completely. "Yes, a dangerous man,
Senor Keogh, a fanatic. Not content with getting rid
of the English, he and his friends turned on their own
leaders, plunged their country into civil war of
the worst kind. As a matter of interest, the Irish Government is anxious to have you back, but only to face
a firing squad. The statement I have received from
them particularly refers to an affair in the town of
Drumdoon four months ago when you ambushed a
vehicle in which four highranking Free State officers
were travelling and killed them all."

The heart seemed to stop inside of me, the throat
dry as what I had tried to keep down all this
long while forced its way to the surface.

"One of them was your elder brother, I understand.
Colonel Sean Keogh."

I was aware of van Horne's startled glance, swayed

forward and grabbed at the edge of the desk as the walls undulated. "You go to hell, you bastard," I told Bonilla.

"Your own destination, my friend. You and the good father here were both sentenced to death by a military court this afternoon. You will be shot in the morning."

He stood up and walked out without a word and I stayed, leaning heavily on the edge of the desk, fighting for air.

There was a hand under my elbow. Van Horne said quietly, "Are you all right? Can you make it?"

"No sympathy," I said.

"That word doesn't figure in my vocabulary." As I turned to look at him, the craggy, used-up face broke into a smile that was like no smile I'd seen on top of earth. Courage and strength. Genuine strength and infinite compassion.

"We will go now, señores," I heard Cordona say, polite for the first time and only because we were dead men walking.

Van Horne said softly, "You will walk out of here on your own two feet and smile. Do you understand me, boy?"

My grandfather all over again, but he was right and let it be so. I would not disgrace my name this night or any other. I took a deep breath to steady myself and went through the french windows ahead of them all.

It was cold in the cell, bitterly cold and the stench of the place seemed worse than ever after our brief visit to the outside world. I stood at the window, staring into the night. After a while, the key rattled in the lock again, the door opened and Cordona reappeared with a couple of packets of Artistas and a straw-covered bottle of tequila. He put them down on the floor and went out without a word.

Van Horne said, "Well, I'll be damned, even that bastard has a heart. Here, take a pull at this."

He passed me the tequila bottle. As I have said, I never did care for the stuff, but it was warming if nothing else. I took a couple of swallows and gave it back to him.

He said, "Do you want to talk about it?"

Now here is a strange thing. I had known him play-acting the priest, I had seen him as another kind of man entirely after the shooting at Tacho's, but this calm, worldly-wise, compassionate man was someone else again. Even the manner of speech had altered.

"How many different people are you, for God's sake?" I demanded.

"Oh, it amuses me to confuse people, but that isn't answering my question."

"All right," I said. "But it's soon told. My brother was six years older than me. He joined the Dublin Fusiliers in 1914, and went to fight England's wars for her, a habit Irishmen find hard to break. He was commissioned in the field, invalided out as a captain at the beginning of 1918."

"Were his politics the same colour as yours?"

"I think you could say that. He rose to command a Flying Column in spite of his bad right leg. We parted company over the treaty, with the English. He was one of those, like Collins, who thought we'd suffered enough. That half-a-loaf was better than nothing."

"And you were a die-hard Republican."

I couldn't see his face, so dark had it become, which was perhaps a good thing. I said, "I didn't know he was in the car that day in Drumdoon. We were expecting the divisional commander."

"These things happen in war."

"I killed him," I said. "Killed all four of them neatly and expeditiously with a Thompson gun from the upstairs window of Cohan's Select Bar. It was raining hard at the time and not a soul on the streets. They knew better. The purpose of terrorism is to terrorise, that's what Mick Collins used to say and I believed him. In the end, it was too late to change. Even after Drumdoon. All I could do was run for the hills."

"It's never too late for anything in this life."

"Now you're playing priest again."

He changed, just like that. "Damn me, but you're right, Keogh, and that won't do at all. Seems to me a man ought to stand by what he's been, even at the final end of things, or his whole life's been nothing."

"That's me," I said. "A perfect description."

"Oh, I don't know. What about that Indian kid. You saved her bacon back there at Tacho's didn't you? That ought to count for something."

There was a kind of comfort in that and I thought of her for a moment, the dark, calm eyes, the olive skin, the warmth of her body when she had held me close on that night of torrential rain.

"I'd say she owes as much to you as she does to me," I said. "If you hadn't taken a hand in the game when you did . . ."

"Don't make the mistake of assigning a motive to my conduct that didn't exist, Keogh." His voice was harsh again, his old cynical self. "I didn't intend anything when I stepped into the bar at Tacho's that night. What took place just happened to be the way things worked out. There was no method intended in my madness. And now, I've talked enough. I'm going to sleep."

He relieved himself into the bucket in the corner, then lay on his straw mattress, his irons chinking as he arranged his legs.

I stayed there at the window, clutching the bars and staring up into the cold night sky at stars older than time itself, that would be still here tomorrow night when little Emmet Keogh was long gone. God help me, but looking back on it all, this rag of a life of mine, it seemed such a pitiful waste.

The sergeant of the guard brought us coffee at seven o'clock, but no food, which was reasonable enough under the circumstances.

After that, we were left alone for a good two hours. Van Horne had nothing to say. In the cold morning light he looked older than his years and his beard was tangled, the face dirty. I can have been in no better case and was feeling understandably depressed. The sounds of activity in the courtyard outside didn't help.

There was the tramp of marching feet, a shouted order or two and van Horne got to his feet and went to the window. There was a certain amount of confused shouting and then a high-pitched scream.

"What's going on?" I demanded.

"They're getting ready to shoot some poor bastard and he isn't taking it too well."

I joined him at the window and peered through the bars. There was a wooden post in front of the wall on the other side of the courtyard and the prisoner they were tying to it was struggling so hard that it was taking four soldiers to control him. As they moved away leaving him upright against the post, I got a look at his face and could not avoid a short, ironic laugh.

"As old Tacho said, sometimes God looks down through the clouds."

"You know him?"

I nodded. "Captain José Ortiz. Chief of Police in Bonito."

"Well, I'll be damned," van Horne said. "Bonilla certainly doesn't let the grass grow under his feet."

Ortiz was unable to disgrace himself further for they had gagged him with an old bandanna and blindfolded him. Cordona was in charge of the execution and I stayed to watch for some perverse reason of my own, but then I had seen a great many men die this way in my time and there was no reality to it at all. A single sharp command, a ragged volley and the pitiful creature strapped to the post ceased to exist. No satisfaction to be had there and in any event, as I turned away they came for us.

We were taken by the sergeant and half-a-dozen men through the cell block into a cool, white-walled corridor with windows so high that one could not see out into the courtyard. The sergeant produced a key and removed our leg irons, and we waited.

After a while, the door opened behind us and I could tell by the rattle of leg irons on the floor that another prisoner was being brought up. I looked over my shoulder casually and got the shock of my life. Janos was standing there between two guards, his linen suit filthy beyond description, sweat oozing from that great fat face.

His eyes widened and without the slightest hint of embarrassment he said, "Why, Mr. Keogh, sir. We meet again."

The effrontery of the man was such that I was unable to contain my laughter. "Meet my good friend Mr. Janos from Bonito," I said to van Horne.

"The character who confuses whisky with guns?" Van Horne gave him a hard smile. "At least you'll present them with a sizable target, my friend."

Janos ignored him. They had still left him his stick and he stumped forward as the leg irons were removed. "Mr. Keogh. I feel this whole sorry business very deeply. My fault, sir. If I could make amends I would, believe me. If it is any satisfaction, we are to suffer the same fate."

"No satisfaction at all," I told him.

The door opened and the Lieutenant Cordona entered, a sheaf of papers in his right hand. He nodded to the sergeant who took Janos by the arm and led him forward.

"Paul Janos," Cordona said, reading from the first sheet. "Age fifty-nine, otherwise Count Rakossy, sometime Colonel of the Austrian Imperial Guards."

"Must we really rake up all that sort of thing?" Janos said wearily.

"You have been tried by a military tribunal on the charge of treason against the state and have been found guilty as charged. The sentence of the court is that you be shot to death."

"Then I would suggest that we get it over with as quickly as possible."

Cordona saluted formally and opened the door. Janos turned and said gravely, "I am sorry I got you into this mess, Mr. Keogh, and that's the truth of it, sir. Good luck."

The impudence of the man was breathtaking and when he went out through the door it was as if he were taking them and not the other way round.

It was over very quickly. A shouted command, the fusillade, a single revolver shot and no more than a couple of minutes after that the door opened and Cordona and his men returned.

They took van Horne, the sergeant and half-a-dozen

men closing in on him before we knew what was happening as if they anticipated trouble.

As they pushed him through the door, he turned and called over his shoulder. "No regrets, Keogh."

Which put a lump in my throat the size of my fist. I closed my eyes and waited, the coldness seeping through me. The inevitability of death is something few men ever consciously consider for to do so would make life itself unbearable, but now, in a real and frightening way, I knew that I was going to die. That I had only a few more minutes to live.

The rifles crashed outside and I stayed there, eyes closed, listening to the marching feet as they approached the door. When I opened them again, Cordona was before me, the final scrap of paper in his hand.

"Emmet Keogh, age twenty-four, British citizen . . ."

His voice droned on and I looked beyond him out into the terrace at his side of the courtyard, the hard black shadows of the pillars falling across the flagstones like iron bars in the morning sun. And then we were moving out through the door and across the courtyard to the wooden post, blood fresh on the cobbles at its base.

I stood quietly while they strapped my ankles, waist and chest. Cordona said gravely, "I regret the absence of a priest, señor. You must make your peace with God in your own way."

Then they fastened a bandanna about my eyes and walked away. My mind seemed frozen. It was as if this was happening to someone else, not me. I didn't even feel fear any more, could think of no prayer worth the saying.

He gave the order to load and it was as if I could hear each bolt click home separately for they were not particularly well trained or perhaps they had no stomach for the work.

His voice brought them to the ready. There was a single breathtaking moment in which I begged my brother to forgive me and then an ear-shattering roll as they fired.

I was still alive, that much was obvious, had not even been hit, which made no kind of sense at all. There was silence for a moment and then steps approached. The bandanna was untied and I blinked in the sudden glare of the sun.

Cordona was pale, but calm. "You will come with me now, señor," he said impassively.

The sergeant was busy with my straps and I moistened my lips and croaked, "What in the name of God are you playing at, Lieutenant?"

He turned without a word and led off across the courtyard and the sergeant applied the butt of his rifle gently in the small of my back and sent me after him. We went through the archway into that small enclosed garden again. There was no sign of Bonilla but Oliver van Horne and Janos stood against the wall, guarded by three soldiers.

I paused, staring at them in astonishment and Janos called, "You are familiar with Alice in Wonderland, sir? Curiouser and curiouser was the phrase she used as I recall."

Van Horne said nothing, his face grim like any predatory animal sensing danger and we were given no opportunity for further conversation for Cordona went straight in through the french windows and the sergeant brought the three of us after him.

Colonel Bonilla was sitting behind his desk enjoying a late breakfast. He glanced up, wiping his mouth

with a napkin and nodded to Cordona who ordered
the sergeant and his men outside and took up position
by the window.

"An unpleasant start to the day, gentlemen," Bonilla
observed. "But one which I trust makes the point that
I hold you all in the hollow of my hand."

It was van Horne who broke the silence. "All right,
so you could be Lord High executioner if you wanted
to be. You've made your point. What's it all about?
What's the game?"

"A good word for it," Bonilla said. "Rather apt, but
it's really quite simple. I want you, Senor van Horne,
to play the priest again, something you seem to have a
talent for."

Van Horne stared at him in amazement. "What did
you say?"

"And Señor Janos will make an excellent businessman. He has the build for it. He looks substan-
tial therefore people will believe he is in other ways."

"I am complimented, sir," Janos told him with considerable irony.

Bonilla ignored him. "And you, Señor Keogh. Your
task is the simplest of all. It might have been created
especially for a man of your peculiarly dark talents."

He smiled gravely. "All you have to do is kill someone for me."

SIX

"In the year since the Revolution there has been much unrest, much violence in many parts of Mexico, but nowhere more so than in this area. Worst of all is Mojada in the northern foothills of the Sierra Madre."

Bonilla indicated the right spot on the map with the end of his riding crop and I took a close look. It was perhaps thirty or forty miles from Huila, the sort of place that had sprung up a couple of centuries earlier at the side of the old pack trails across the mountains.

"All right, so what's the story?" van Horne demanded.

"It is soon told, señor. I am military governor for this entire area based on Huila and yet a bare thirty miles away, there is not only no law and order, but a state of complete anarchy that none of my predecessors succeeded in doing anything about."

I said, "I thought that's what you had troops for?"

"I have two hundred men to police the whole of my command area. An army would not be enough to handle the situation in Mojada and the few I have been able to spare in the past have never succeeded in achieving anything. You see, gentlemen, the key to the whole affair is to be found in the personality of one remarkable man, Tomás de la Plata, once a major un-

der my own command until he turned his back
on honour."

He said the last bit as if it really meant something
to him and continued, "Once, the De la Platas were
great landowners in these parts. Now, all that is left
is a decaying hacienda outside Mojada and a few acres
of land plus an old silver mine that hasn't been worked
in ten or twelve years."

"Does anyone still live there?" I asked.

"His father, Don Angel de la Plata and his sister,
Chela."

"And Tomás? What about him?"

"God alone knows where he is from one moment to
the next. Last month he and his men robbed the night
express to Madera. Not content with that, he shot the
driver and left the train to free-wheel down a gradient.
It ran off the track after five miles. Over thirty people
were killed, many injured."

"And he can still find people to follow him after that?" van Horne said.

"Death and suffering has been the story of my country for years now, señor. It has become something of a
way of life to us. Three million dead in the Revolution
alone. What are thirty more compared to that?"

"Fair enough," I said. "But I still can't get a clear
picture of the man in my own mind. What is he? Dissatisfied revolutionary or plain bandit?"

"God alone knows and Tomás himself." Bonilla
carefully fitted a cigarette into a black, ivory holder.
"When I first knew him he was just out of university.
The complete idealist. Everything was wrong, therefore everything had to be changed."

"Which can hardly have made him popular with
people of his own class, surely," Janos put in.

"No, he lost a great deal by aligning himself with the people and their cause so completely. Even his own father publicly disowned him."

"But he didn't mind," I said. "All for the cause. He sounds familiar."

Bonilla smiled rather sadly. "It has been my experience that idealists of this type tend to be complete fanatics who cannot tolerate less than perfection either in the cause they fight for, or in the conduct of their associates."

"Perfection is hard to come by in this world," van Horne said.

"Life, on the whole, is something of a compromise between what we would like and what we can have. Tomás was never capable of making that kind of accommodation."

"So what exactly went wrong in the end?" I asked.

"A great mystery. On the successful conclusion of the Revolution, Tomás was transferred to Huila because of his special knowledge of the area and made second-in-command to the then military governor, a Colonel Varga. It seems they didn't get on very well."

"Any particular reason?"

"Varga was a great ox of a man, a peon who had risen through the ranks. A good soldier in his own rough way, but still inclined to eat with his fingers, if you follow me. He was found in bed one morning with his throat cut from ear to ear. He had also been deprived of his manhood, a macabre touch if you like."

"And Tomás de la Plata?"

"Gone, señor, vanished from the face of the earth, to re-appear a month later at the head of twenty or thirty rogues who attacked and robbed a military supply column on its way here. The first of many such acts of lawlessness."

"And where does he get the men from?" van Horne asked.

"There are always those dissatisfied after every revolution, as Señor Keogh knows better than anyone from his own country." Which was hitting pretty low. "Just as there are always those who will reject any kind of authority if they can. In the area of Mojada, the people enjoy complete freedom from state control. Taxes are not collected for no tax collector can operate. There is no law, no justice because no police officer can live there. They have even rejected the church. Three priests during the past eighteen months. Two murdered and one found wandering in the desert, stripped of his clothes, beaten half to death. Quite out of his mind."

To my surprise, van Horne made no comment to that one and it was Janos who said, "Are you saying that De la Plata actually uses Mojada as his headquarters with the active support of the people?"

"Let us say he is to be found in that general area most of the time and occasionally in Mojada itself although it is no secret that there are always a few of his followers on view, just to keep the general population in line."

"So most people up there don't particularly care for him?" I said.

"They fear him, señor. I have visited the place on three occasions myself. I have quartered troops there for a month at a time and all we meet is a wall of silence."

"All right, Colonel," van Horne said. "Let's get down to cases. What's all this leading up to?"

"Ten years of war, gentlemen, three million dead, the economy ruined. My country has suffered enough. Now we need stability and quiet, an end to killing.

There is no room for men like Tomás de la Plata. The longer he survives the more the disaffected will seek to join him in the mountains and that won't do at all. I want his head."

"And you expect us to get it for you?" van Horne said.

"If you do, señor, you can have your freedom and the contents of a certain Gladstone bag. Señor Janos may have his hotel back, which would have otherwise been confiscated by the state."

"And me?" I said. "What about me."

He eyed me speculatively and then sighed. "Why you will be free to go to hell in your own way, Señor Keogh."

A thought I hardly found pleasant. Janos made the obvious point. "And what is to prevent us from simply clearing off into the blue, sir, once we leave here? Why go to Mojada at all?"

"Because you have nowhere to go, señores. Not one of you. How far would you get. One hundred miles? Two? And next time there would be no choice. I have not only taken you out of the jaws of death, I have given you a chance of surviving with something in hand. I had thought you all intelligent men, whatever else you are."

Van Horne turned to look at me enquiringly, then Janos. He said, "All right, Colonel, we're in. What's the plan?"

Bonilla showed no emotion at all for, as it soon became clear, the fact that we might refuse had never entered his calculations.

"I told you there was a silver mine on the De la Plata land. For some time now the old man has been trying to interest one mining company after the other in the idea of working the mine again on a partnership basis. He is very short of money."

"Doesn't Tomás help out?"

"He and his father have never been reconciled although he visits the hacienda frequently to see his sister, Chela. They have always been very close."

"So what about this mining thing?" van Horne demanded.

"No one will play because of the unsettled nature of the country. I know this because as all mail for the area passes through Huila, I have been privileged to read the various letters. I decided to take a hand in the game myself the day before yesterday and forwarded a letter to old De la Plata in your name, Señor Janos."

"Did you, by God," Janos exclaimed.

"You will be interested to know that you represent the Herrara Mining Company of Mexico City and will be arriving at Mojada to inspect the property within the next few days, together with your assistant. Your previous experience should prove useful, Mr. Keogh."

"You think of everything," I said.

"I need to, my friend. I have been a soldier a long time. Survival has become something of a habit."

Van Horne leaned across the desk, helped himself to a cigar from the box at Bonilla's elbow. "You've left me to the last, Colonel, so it must be good."

Cordona took a quick, impatient step forward, but Bonilla waved him back, struck a match and gave van Horne a light. "They need a priest in Mojada very badly, Father. I think you would suit them admirably."

Van Horne's face was extraordinarily calm. "Two priests dead and one mad, isn't that the record up there?"

"True, but it does give you an excellent reason for being there which is highly important. Strangers are usually taken to be government spies and treated accordingly. A priest and two mining experts visiting Don Angel at his own request stand some chance of survival, especially when all three are gringos. As some sort of support in case of need, I am sending Lieutenant Cordona with twenty men to Huanca which is some fifteen miles from Mojada in the foothills of the mountains. We frequently use the abandoned *rancheria* there as a base for patrol activity in the area so his presence will excite no particular comment.

I said, "What about Tomás? When is he supposed to show up?"

"He will know you are in the area within a matter of hours just as he will know the nature of your business with his father. I think we may take it for granted that he will put in an appearance at the hacienda without too much delay to find out for himself what exactly is going on. After all, the possibility of the mine being put to work again is certain to be of more than passing interest to him."

"Why not just send us back out to the stake and have done with it, Colonel," I said. "Mojada is just as certain."

"Hell it is," van Horne cut in. "This way depends on us and no one else. Jesus, boy, didn't you take on the whole bloody British army and beat them at their own game? Well, no bunch of greasy peons with their backsides hanging out is going to put me under the sod. I'll go to Mojada for you, Colonel. I'll even play priest for you again, but anyone who tries to blow my head off will get the hardest sermon of his life. Understand?"

"Perfectly." Bonilla stood up. "I would prefer Tomás de la Plata alive, but will accept him dead as long as you provide me with his corpse. A necessary encouragement for the local population." He turned to Janos. "You may use the Mercedes. It should go well with your new role and a lift to an impoverished priest with the same destination would be an act of kindness no one could quarrel with."

"A real nice thought, Colonel," van Horne said with some irony. "Anyone can see your heart is in the right place."

"Lieutenant Cordona will conduct you to more comfortable quarters elsewhere. He will also take care of all your requirements. I wish you luck, gentlemen." Which was a reasonably polite way of dismissing us and as he also sat down and busied himself with some papers, he made his point pretty thoroughly.

Cordona led the way out through the french windows into the garden. He dismissed the sergeant and his men, then carried on without even checking to see whether we were following him.

On the far side of the garden, a door opened into a small, quieter courtyard with a covered terrace on three sides and another fountain splashing across blue and white tiles in the centre. It was cool and pleasant and remote and the sounds of life from the town beyond the wall might have been from another world, which may have been something of an exaggeration, but the contrast between this and what I had been exposed to for the past few days could not have been greater.

As I discovered later, the rooms which surrounded the little courtyard were officers' quarters and Cordona didn't approve. In fact I would say it was all he could do to contain his rage, especially where van Horne was concerned.

He and I had to share and Janos was in the next room on his own. They were both identical. Two beds in each together with the bare essentials of bedroom furniture, whitewashed walls, the complete absence of any kind of religious images, an indication of the anti-clerical line events were taking at that time.

"There is a bath at the end of the row," Cordona said. "With an orderly in charge. When you are ready, he will see that hot water is brought, also anything else you may require."

"Well now, I'd like a woman myself," van Horne told him. "Not too young. Around thirty, black hair, someone who knows what it's all about."

A deliberate attempt to upset Cordona and nothing more, for in all the time I knew van Horne, one noticeable thing about him was his lack of interest in the opposite sex. It almost worked. Cordona's face went very, very white and his hand dropped to the butt of his revolver and for some stray, perverse reason that made no sense to me, I felt sorry for him.

The moment passed. He took a deep breath. "Clothing and various personal belongings that you may need have been provided for you, señor," he said to van Horne, "something extra."

The cassock which van Horne had been wearing until our capture lay on the bed, washed and ironed from the look of it, the shovel hat on top. The Gladstone bag was there, too, although it contained, as it turned out, only the Thompson gun and its spare ammunition clips, the money being elsewhere. On the floor was a black steamer trunk which Cordona nudged with his toe.

"We haven't had a priest here for several months.

The last one died of blackwater fever. This trunk contains his belongings, particularly the vestments and other things you will need to sustain your role."

"Of which you don't approve, I take it?"

"Señor," Cordona said calmly. "If I had my way, I would see you burn in hell before I even allowed you to open this trunk which belonged to a good and kind man. A man of God who died serving his people."

He turned and walked out abruptly and van Horne stayed exactly where he was, staring out of the door, a strange, set expression on his face and then he laughed and slapped his thigh.

"You know, I expected to be dead by now. Isn't life the strangest damn game you ever did play, Keogh?"

A thought, certainly, and I moved to my bed and discovered not only the Enfield in its shoulder holster, but the two suitcases I had last seen in my room at the Hotel Blanca in Bonita.

Janos said, "Only one thing interests me at the moment, gentlemen. The bath and the copious quantities of hot water mentioned."

"Don't you think we should discuss things first?" I said.

"What in the hell is there to discuss?" van Horne put in. "Anything could happen and probably will when we get to Mojada. They might even shoot us on sight. This kind of game is a lot like poker, Keogh. You play it according to the way the cards fall."

"I couldn't agree more," Janos said. "I should have thought this morning an admirable object lesson on the follies of thinking on the possibilities of tomorrow. But the pleasures of the bath call, gentlemen. I shall see you later."

"You could certainly do with it, fat man," van Horne observed.

The Hungarian produced two feet of steel from inside the black ivory walking stick and had the point nudging van Horne under the chin before he knew what was happening.

"You were jesting, of course, sir." Janos smiled good-humouredly.

Van Horne raised a hand. "That's all I wanted to know, Count whatever-your-name-is."

Janos rammed the sword back into place and chuckled. "By God, sir, but you're a character. I can see we're going to get along."

Someone else he was going to deal famously with. He left, his great frame shaking and van Horne said, "Now there's a man I very definitely would prefer to have for me rather than against me."

He got down on his knees and opened the steamer trunk. The first thing he took out was a cope in faded green that looked as if it had seen many years of service. That was for ordinary use, of course. There was also one in tarnished gold for important feast days and a third in regulation sombre black for requiem mass.

There was a silver chalice carefully wrapped in a piece of old blanket. A ciborium containing the Host, a silver pyx on a chain, holy oils in small silver vials, a thurible, incense. Finally, he discovered a religious image of some sort, very carefully wrapped in several layers of woollen cloth. It was perhaps two feet high and was obviously very old, being carved from wood and hand-painted. It was a remarkable piece of work by any standard and van Horne looked at it for quite some time in silence.

"Who is it?" I said.

"At a guess, I'd say St. Martin de Porres, mainly because he's the only coloured saint I can think of right now. He was illegitimate. The son of an Indian woman and a conquistador. If ever there was a saint for the poor and the downtrodden, I'd say it was he."

Strange how it all came back to me, my boyhood at Knockbree and the scarlet cassock and white cotta of the acolyte that I had hated so much to wear, the horror I felt as my turn approached to serve week-day mass. I was never particularly religious by persuasion and had not been helped by the fact that my grandfather in his old age, and to the great scandal of the country, had forsworn his religion and joined the Plymouth Brethren which made life, as he constantly told me, considerably more comfortable.

But I had long since ceased to believe in any kind of a God of comfort. The only God I had ever known was a God of wrath who brought violence and anger, rage in heaven, not love, and I could manage very well without him.

Van Horne replaced the statue in the trunk, closed the lid slowly and looked up. "It looks as if I'm in business, doesn't it Keogh?" he said, but he was not smiling.

I had half-an-hour in the tub after Janos, wallowing in the water so hot that it almost took the skin off me, then I made way for van Horne, returned to our room with a towel round my waist and dressed in clean clothes, thanks to the suitcases Bonilla had thoughtfully provided.

I found Janos seated at a large, round table on the shaded terrace on the other side of the courtyard. An Indian orderly danced attendance and the table was loaded with good things. Tortillas, frijoles, a great plate of anchovies, green olives—never a favourite of mine—and sweetcorn cooked in butter. There was also fresh fruit and several bottles of red wine.

Janos ate surprisingly little but drank a great deal and seemed disposed to talk. I had little doubt about my ability to pose as a mining surveyor or engineer and told him so, which appeared to satisfy him. We decided between us that his own role would be that of the non-specialist financier interested merely in the economics of the thing. In other words, a good, solid businessman.

By this time, he was into his second bottle of wine and had grown considerably more loquacious. "A dangerous enterprise, sir. A dangerous enterprise, but we shall come through, never fear. Your friend, van Horne, is obviously a man of parts and you, sir . . . why you remind me of myself when young. Quicksilver."

God knows how I kept myself from laughing out loud for he leaned across, as serious as you please and said, "Glands, sir, Glands. Nature's curse since I was thirty-one years of age. Until then I was normal as the next man, a cavalry officer of distinction, bearer of an ancient name and now—all gone. All gone." He snorted like an old bull and to my amazement there were tears in his eyes and then his chin dropped to his chest and he started to snore.

I left him to it, lit a cigarette and went for a walk. The garden outside Bonilla's quarters was deserted and so was the main courtyard where the morning executions, fake or otherwise, had taken place.

I wandered across to the stake to which I had been strapped, examined the bullet-scared wall behind and wondered, and not for the first time, what life was all about. Certainly an affair over which few human beings had any kind of control.

I turned and sauntered towards the main gates which were great, iron-barred affairs, now closed, through which I could see into the street beyond. It was only as I got close that I realised a soldier leaned negligently on his rifle in the sentry post which had been hollowed out of the thickness of the wall in the archway. He opened half-closed eyes, blinked as I approached and straightened warily. I nodded, bade him good evening and peered out through the bars casually.

The street was deserted except for two Indians sitting against the wall of an adobe house opposite. The man wore rawhide leggings and a red flannel shirt, his shoulder-length hair bound with a band of the same material. He cradled an old Winchester repeating rifle in his lap.

The woman had hair as black as any raven's wing, a dark curtain to her shoulders, a scarlet band around her head. Her shirt, heavily embroidered with Indian-work, was also of scarlet and the belt at her waist was of hand-beaten silver. A black skirt fell to just below her knee and as she stood up, I saw that she wore boots of untanned leather underneath.

She ran across the street, reached in through the bars and grabbed for my hands. It took me several seconds to realise that this proud, barbaric little beauty was Victoria Balbuena.

I held on tight, aware of emotions I couldn't explain even to myself as I looked down into her face, the eyes that tried to speak for the voice could not.

"It's all right," I said. "I'm fine. There's nothing to worry about."

The sentry had me out of the way with a quick, unexpected shove and drove the butt of his rifle at those small, brown hands in a blow of such savagery that any kind of contact would have crippled her.

She got her hands out through the bars just in time and, as the rifle butt rang against the iron, I had him

by the throat and started to squeeze, a black rage in
me so strong I was close to ending him.

There was a certain amount of confused shouting.
I was aware of the Indian with the white hair at her
shoulder, the lever of the Winchester clicking as he
put a round into the breech and then van Horne was
somehow between me and the sentry forcing us apart.

The sentry ended up back against the wall on one
knee and started to raise his rifle and Cordona arrived
on the run to kick it from his grasp. The unfortunate
sentry tried to stand and went down again, the lieutenant's fist in his mouth.

I helped the poor devil to his feet, propping him
against the wall, but when I turned, Victoria and her
companion had disappeared.

"Where did she go?" I grabbed at the bars. "Did you
see who it was?"

Van Horne nodded. "I told you about Yaquis, boy.
She's reverted to type. Gone back to her own kind."

Cordona nodded. "The man she was with, Nachita,
he is an elder of the Wind River Yaqui, her mother's
tribe. Twice a year he comes to Huila, leading a pack
train over the mountain. Only the Yaqui dare do such
work these days."

"But what was she doing with him? Why was she
dressed like that?"

"He noticed her sitting outside the gate here
the other day, recognised the Yaqui blood and questioned her. To these people, family ties are all important and he and the girl are of the same blood. Her
mother was his cousin. I questioned him closely on this
yesterday."

So, she had found her own people after all in spite
of events. I said slowly, "Will she be all right?"

"To these people, descent is through the mother so

the girl is considered wholly Yaqui and her mother's father was clan chief, which makes her a person of much status. Very important in every way. They will be honoured to have her back amongst them. Believe me I know these people. This man, Nachita, and his men would have the eyes of any man who even looked at her in the wrong way."

"Like I told you, Keogh," van Horne said. "Yaqui are worse than Apache."

But I turned and walked quickly away, aware of the strange, illogical hurt in me. It made no kind of sense—none at all. When I stretched out on my bed and closed my eyes, her face rose to haunt me. Not beautiful, yet more beautiful than any I had known in my life before.

I slept for three or four hours, waking just before ten o'clock according to an old tin alarm clock at the side of the bed.

There was no sign of van Horne, but when I opened the door and looked out into the courtyard, I saw that he and Janos were sitting at the table on the other side playing cards in the diffused lemon glow of an oil lamp.

I felt restless and slightly depressed and certainly not at all in the mood for company, so I skirted the edge of the courtyard, keeping to the shadows and went into the garden.

There was no sign of Bonilla and his quarters were in darkness so I had the place to myself. The air was fresh after the heat of the day, a slight wind blowing the fountain in a silver spray and a nearly-full moon was hooked into a cypress tree, black against a curtain of stars.

It was very peaceful and beyond the wall in the

town, a guitar played and someone sang softly. Picture-book Mexico, just the stuff for the tourists. The breeze ruffled the cypress trees again and something moved with it, a dark wraith that had an arm round my throat like magic, a knife blade gleaming dully before my eyes.

The voice was like dry leaves whispering through a forest in the evening. "You will be sensible now, señor, for there is nothing to fear."

Victoria Balbuena stepped out of the shadows. The arm was removed from my throat and she put out her hands to grasp mine. She smiled and it was a smile to turn the night over.

She started to pull me into the shadows and I restrained her. "Hold hard, there, where are we going?"

The eyes were eloquent, but it was Nachita who spoke for her. "We will go now, señor, leave Huila to-night. By dawn we will already be into the mountains and in that country, no *federale* known to man can catch a Yaqui. In four days you will be safe in the Wind River country."

"But why?" I said.

"Because my lady wishes it."

It was the nearest he could come to expressing her status in Spanish and certainly seemed to indicate that Cordona had known what he was talking about.

I held Victoria's hands very lightly and shook my head. "It isn't possible."

Nachita said, "This morning you faced death at the stake, señor, tonight you live. This is an interesting turn of events."

He had a remarkable face and I think it was then that I really noticed him for the first time, directly confronting him as it were. Straight-nosed, thin-lipped with pale brown skin. Full of strength, intelligence and calm pride. I was even more impressed when I discovered later that he was seventy-two years of age.

I said, "Three lives for one. Colonel Bonilla gave me and my two comrades ours in exchange for that of a man named Tomás de la Plata."

He said calmly, "But De Plata still lives, señor, all men know this."

"We're going to Mojada tomorrow to try to remedy that."

"Then you go to a bad end," he said simply.

Victoria had me in a grip like iron. I leaned close and said deliberately, "There is honour in this. Van Horne saved us both at Tacho's, you as well as me. Should I desert him now?"

God alone knows why I came up with that one, but she took it seriously and nodded, her hands going slack in mine. I reached out to touch her cheek, she turned her face sideways and kissed the palm of my hand. About her neck she was wearing a round silver amulet of Indian workmanship on the end of a plaited leather thong. With a sudden, quick gesture, she took it off, pulled it over my head and down around my neck, then reached up, kissed me in a thoroughly European way, turned and disappeared into the darkness.

Nachita said, "I know Mojada, señor, it is an unfilled grave. Think again."

"It is another step along the way, my friend," I told him. "I never go back to anything. Look after her."

He vanished, melted in the shadows as if he had never been and I stood there, fingering the silver amulet, quite unaware of its significance, a great sadness on me as if now, at last, I was at the final bitter end of things and had nothing.

SEVEN

We left at six o'clock on as grey and dreary a morning as you could wish for. A bad omen or perhaps that was just the Celt in me. Van Horne, who had been busy with the cards and wine until the small hours, looked about a hundred years old, although Janos seemed much the same.

Cordona was there to see us off, the boots and uniform absolute perfection, every inch the soldier, even at that time in the morning. He told us he would be leaving with his patrol for the *rancheria* at Huanca later in the day and wished us luck in his usual tight, reserved way. It was obvious that he never expected to see us alive again, which was a cheerful thought on which to depart.

I drove and van Horne sat beside me leaving the rear seat to Janos, who took up space for two men anyway. The streets were quite deserted as we drove through Huila and beyond, the road, if road you could call it, vanished into the grey morning in the general direction of the Sierra Madre.

There was a heavy ground mist that made it difficult to see for more than a few yards in any direction although it varied greatly in intensity. About five miles out of Huila, it cleared a little and I caught a glimpse of something moving up ahead, a flash of scarlet.

As we approached, I saw that it was a pack train of a dozen or more heavily laden mules. The Yaqui, Nachita, guarding the rear, the old Winchester in his right hand, the butt against his thigh. There were three other Indians strung out along the train, hard, dangerous-looking men in head bands and red flannel shirts like a uniform, armed to the teeth and ready to take on the world.

Victoria Balbuena rode at the head of the procession, dressed exactly as when I had last seen her in the garden with the addition of a cloak of some kind of animal fur which hung from around her shoulders against the cold.

I drove past very slowly and Nachita raised the Winchester a foot or so as if in greeting, but Victoria stared straight ahead into the morning, giving no sign, a fierce little queen ignoring the commoners.

At least it brought van Horne to life. "Well, I'll be damned," he said. "I said she'd reverted to type, but this is ridiculous."

About fifty yards further on I pulled into the side of the road and switched off the engine. "Now what are you playing at?" he demanded.

I ignored him, jumped out and ran back into the mist. There was an ornamental bell around the neck of her horse, I heard that first and then she seemed to float into view.

She showed no surprise, no emotion at all to find me standing there. The man closest to her urged his mount forward and Nachita called to him sharply in his own language. Victoria kept on moving, staring straight ahead and I took hold of her stirrup leather and walked beside her. When we reached the Mercedes I released my grip and she kept on going, still without a glance.

The pack train, Nachita bringing up the rear, vanished into the mist. Janos said, "What was that all about?"

I climbed back behind the wheel. As I leaned forward, the silver amulet she had given me swung free and van Horne reached out to examine it.

"She gave you that?"

"And what if she did?"

He laughed harshly. "Let me tell you about the Yaqui, boy, Some of their clans put the womenfolk first. Why it's even the woman who chooses the man. Each girlchild at birth is given the symbol of her sex and power by her mother in the form of a silver amulet. When a girl wants a husband, she simply puts her amulet on him. When she wants a divorce, she takes it back."

For some reason, the whole thing seemed to strike him as extremely humourous. "Damn me, Keogh, but you've just been to the altar and didn't know it."

He laughed so hard I thought it likely he might do himself an injury and Janos joined in. Strange, but I saw nothing funny about the business at all.

"So what?" I said. "I'll likely be dead meat in a day or two. We all will."

Which wiped the smile from both faces very effectively, and I drove away.

Within another hour, the grey skies had lifted, the mist dispersed and the sun was climbing high into the heavens. The semi-desert plain we drove through was a dun-coloured haze rising into the mountains, the canyons dark with shadow.

If ever there was country not intended for the automobile it was this and, although the Mercedes was built like a tank and could obviously stand a great deal of punishment, there seemed no point in asking for trouble, so I drove with extreme caution for most of the way. Indeed there were occasions, especially as we started to climb into the mountains, when it was necessary to get out and clear particularly large rocks out of the way.

Naturally, Janos was of no help at all in this kind of situation and he sat in the rear seat, smoking a cigar and commiserating with us loudly. Amazingly, van Horne took this quite well. In fact he grew progressively more cheerful as the morning drew on.

About ten miles out of Mojada, we stopped and had what amounted to a picnic for food had been provided in a basket carrier. Cold meat, anchovies, olives and fresh bread and a couple of bottles of red wine.

It was all rather gay and Janos toasted the general direction of Mojada, glass raised. "We who are about to die, salute thee."

"Fine sentiments, but not for me," van Horne said. "What about you, Keogh?"

"It comes as God wills," I shrugged. "Isn't that what the bull fighters say just before they go into the plaza?"

It touched something deep inside him, I realise that now looking back on it all, for I think the change was already working in him although it is difficult to say in life where anything begins or ends. Certainly the good humour left him and there was a strange, bleak look on his face as he stood and looked up into the mountains.

"It's a thought, Keogh, a hell of a thought." He shivered quite distinctly and forced a smile. "Strange how cold the wind can be, even in the sun."

And there was no wind blowing.

There were horsemen in the hills as we moved closer

to Mojada. Janos drew my attention to them, but they were far, far above us and it was impossible to see who they were. They kept pace and only dropped out of sight completely when we came over the final rise in the trail and looked down at Mojada in the hollow below.

It was little more than a village, surrounded by a crumbling adobe wall perhaps fifteen feet high, a relic of the days when there had been a constant threat from Indians. Access was gained through an arched gateway and inside, there were thirty or forty adobe *casas*, a small crumbling church with a bell tower that looked as if it had once been whitewashed and what looked like the hotel Cordona had mentioned, if hotel one could call it in such a place.

I negotiated a flock of sheep on the way down, the three old men in charge staring at us in amazement and moved in through the gateway in the wall. Once inside, we were besieged by a dozen or so ragged and barefoot children who ran at the tail of the car. Janos threw a little loose change to scatter them as I pulled up outside the hotel. It was a poor sort of place, the façade crumbling, eroding a little bit more day-by-day in the heat and no one doing anything about it. A board sign over the door said CASA MOJADA.

I got out and opened the rear door for Janos. The children stood in a silent half-circle at a respectable distance, only moving away with considerable reluctance at the urging of four or five women who had appeared from nearby houses.

There were three or four men squatting in the shade of the hotel porch, backs against the wall. Typical peons, poorly clothed and with the weary, lined faces of the prematurely old. Men who had worked like dogs since childhood to keep body and soul together. They had started with nothing and would end the same way.

Inside it was cool and dark. The floor was stone-flagged, there were two or three tables and chairs and a bar counter with a neatly scrubbed top, bottles ranged behind it. There wasn't a customer in sight and no one to serve either. Janos hammered on the counter with his stick, then slumped into a chair, the sweat already pouring from his face again.

There was a sudden, startled gasp, I swung round and found a woman standing in an open doorway to the left of the bar. She was perhaps forty years of age and looked frightened out of her wits at the sight of us. The most significant thing about her was that she was pregnant and at that stage when she could expect the child at any time or I had wasted four years medical training.

A man appeared behind her pulling on a jacket, tall and thin, middle-aged, hair iron-grey as was the large moustache he wore. He muttered something to the woman, pushed her back through the door and came forward.

"At your orders, señores."

"And who might you be?" Janos demanded.

"Rafael Moreno, señor, I run the hotel. I am also mayor of Mojada."

"Is that so." Janos wiped sweat from his face. "My name is Janos and this is my associate, Señor Keogh. We are here at Don Angel de la Plata's invitation to inspect his mine." Moreno didn't seem to be able to think of anything to say and Janos added sharply, "We shall require accommodation man, don't you understand? Two rooms."

At that moment van Horne came in through the door and the look of shock and amazement on Moreno's face had to be seen to be believed. He took an involuntary step backwards and crossed himself briefly.

"This good man, Father van Horne, begged a lift of me when he heard my destination in Huila," Janos told him. "You will perhaps be good enough to direct him to the priest's house."

"The priest's house?" Moreno looked at him in stupefaction. "But there is no priest's house, señor. We do not have a priest in Mojada."

"But you do now, my son," van Horne said with surprising gentleness. "You have a church. Now you have a priest again."

A look of genuine horror appeared on Moreno's face. "We have no priest, Father, it is not permitted." He flung out his arms wildly. "There are no rooms available. The hotel is full, do you understand? You must go away, all of you. And you, Father," he said to van Horne, "you most of all." Then he quite simply walked out, closing the door behind him.

There was a reasonably heavy silence. I went behind the bar, found three glasses and filled them with beer from a stone jug cooling in a bucket of water.

"I should have thought he'd have been warned we were coming," I said.

"Or should have been." Van Horne drank a little of his beer and nodded. "That's more like it. There's a game of sorts being played here."

"Then what, may I ask, is our next move?" Janos said.

"The obvious one under the circumstances. We all play our parts. You two deliver me to the church with my belongings, the courteous thing to do, then you drive out to the hacienda and see Don Angel with your tale of woe. He'll probably offer to put you up."

"Which leaves you on your own," I said.

He smiled gravely and raised his left hand and I saw

that he was holding the Gladstone bag. "Not as long as I've got this," he said. "Now let's get moving."

When we went into the porch at the front of the church the smell of dirt and decay was immediately apparent. The door stood open for the simple reason that the lock had been smashed. Van Horne pushed it back with his boot and led the way in.

The place was a shambles. Wooden benches overturned and smashed, obscene words scrawled in charcoal on the whitewashed walls. There were piles of excrement everywhere and not only the canine variety. Humans had been here also. Even the altar, a plain block of grey stone that looked very ancient had not been missed. As obscene a version of the sexual act as I have ever seen had been chalked on the front.

Van Horne stood looking at it for quite some time, then put out a hand and touched the top of the altar gently. "The poor ignorant fools," he said. "I wonder if they knew what they were doing? The whole place will have to be re-consecrated after this."

He opened a door to one side and led the way into what was obviously the vestry. There was a desk and an old wardrobe, even a narrow iron cot in the corner, although the mattress looked as if it could give one just about every disease known to man.

Van Horne said, "This will do me. Help me in with my trunk, then get started on your end of things."

We brought it in between us and put it down in a corner of the room. I said, "Do you know what you're doing?"

"I usually do. I'll use the blankets from the car and beg a mattress and a lamp from Moreno. He'll hardly refuse me that much."

He seemed abstracted, his eyes moving restlessly

about the tiny church, the great hands clenching and unclenching nervously. I glanced enquiringly at Janos who shrugged and we left him to it and went outside.

"He is taking his part seriously, our friend," Janos observed as he climbed into the rear of the Mercedes

"You think so?" I shrugged. "Oh, I don't know. It's bad enough, what's been done to the place, in all conscience. I wasn't exactly laughing out loud myself."

But I didn't really believe that, not for one moment for I had seen the look on van Horne's face at the desecration of the altar. A kind of agony had showed there for a moment, and his voice had changed again, perhaps the most significant thing of all.

The hacienda was three miles on the other side of Mojada according to the map, and yet we came to the beginning of the land area within a mile, a great archway across a side road with a coat of arms and the name De la Plata carved into the stone.

I drove on through a rolling plain of tawny grassland with here and there, cows bunched together in small groups, usually in the shade of a thicket of cottonwoods.

A mile beyond the archway a shot sounded on the warm air and three horsemen galloped out of a fold in the ground parallel to the dirt road we were following. I kept right on going and the leader levelled a rifle across his left arm and fired again, raising dust no more than a couple of yards in front of us. I did the sensible thing and braked to a halt.

"If you are interested, I obtained a revolver from Cordona before leaving and my ability to shoot straight is one thing my glands haven't altered in the slightest," Janos said calmly as they approached.

"We'll see," I said. "Try laying down the law first."

They were all dressed as working vaqueros in straw sombreros and rawhide leggings, but the one who appeared to be in charge, the man with the rifle, was cast in his own mould. He was about the size of van Horne with a hard, brutal face and the largest hands I have ever seen on any man.

"What do you think you're playing at?" Janos roared.

"This is private land," the other told him in a voice roughened by a great many years of disease and liquor.

"I am here at the express invitation of the owner of this property, Don Angel de la Plata," Janos said crisply.

"You are a bad liar, señor, for I am Raul Jurado, foreman to Don Angel and would be the first to be informed of such a visit."

He raised his left arm bringing the muzzle of his rifle up. My fingers were already touching the butt of the Enfield, but there was no need. Janos said, "You will notice that my hand is inside my coat pocket, my friend, where it holds a loaded revolver. You are a large man and at this range I would have considerable difficulty in missing you."

The barrel of the rifle didn't even flicker and Jurado's face might have been carved from stone. I don't know how it would have gone, but the situation was solved for us by a new arrival.

A voice called, "Jurado, you fool, what are you doing?"

A young woman cantered over the rise and came towards us. She was booted and spurred like a man, wore Spanish riding breeches in black leather, a white silk shirt open at the neck and a Cordoban hat

tilted forward to shade the pale, oval face from the
sun.

"What's going on here? she demanded and struck at
the barrel of Jurado's rifle, knocking it askew.

"Strangers," he said gruffly. "Trespassers."

"Señora, allow me to introduce myself and my companion." Janos stood up and managed a slight bow. He
had style, whatever else you could say about him. "My
name is Paul Janos representing the Herrara Mining
Company and this is Señor Emmet Keogh, a mining engineer. I am here at the express invitation of Don Angel de la Plata and yet for some obscure reason, this
man chose to fire on us."

The girl's face was suddenly contorted with rage,
her arm swept up and the leather thong at the end of
her riding whip slashed across Jurado's face.

"Animal!" she cried. "What are you trying to do?"

He got an arm up to defend himself. "I had my orders, señorita."

"Orders?" she spat the word out as if she didn't like
the taste. "I give the orders here, not my brother. Now
get out of my sight and take my horse with you."

She swung to the ground and flung the reins at him
in a single swift movement. For a moment, I thought
he would argue and then his hand went to the brim of
his sombrero and he turned and cantered away, taking her horse with him, his companions following behind.

The girl removed her hat and I realised at once that
she was older than she had at first appeared. At least
thirty, with a skin so pale that it was almost translucent
and great, dark eyes that seemed to contain all the
tragedy in the world.

"Chela de la Plata at your orders, señores," she said.

"If you will permit me to ride with you, I will guide you to my father's house."

There was a whole complex of stabling and out-buildings of one sort or another, most of which looked to be in a general state of decay. The hacienda itself lay beyond them, a line of cypress trees behind it. It was built in the old colonial style in weathered brown stone, single storeyed and collonaded at the front.

When I stopped the Mercedes at the foot of the broad flight of stone steps, the first thing I noticed were the bullet scars in the pillars and the wall beyond. There had been hard fighting here at one time, so much was evident.

We followed Chela de la Plata up the steps and entered a cool, dark entrance hall with the heads of several bulls mounted on the walls. The great oaken door she opened on the left could also boast a bullet scar or two, but the room was truly delightful. Heavy, eighteenth-century Spanish furniture in black oak, a floor of polished pine with here and there a bright splash of colour from an Indian rug and a great stone fireplace which at the moment contained no fire.

"I will bring my father to you, señores. Please wait here," she said and went out.

"They must have lived in style at one time," Janos said and he sank into a tapestry-covered armchair and looked about him admiringly.

I went to the great window at the far end and looked out. Beyond, there was a garden surrounded by stone walls. Once it must have been quite spectacular, but now it was greatly decayed. One of the saddest things in the world, a garden in decline.

The door clicked open and Chela entered pushing

a wheel chair. The occupant was a frail, sick-looking man with grey hair so long that it almost reached his shoulders. The face bore no resemblance to hers at all for it was long and rather bony with moist brown eyes that seemed to look out at the world in wonder and dismay. He had a rug around his legs and looked, not to put too fine a point on it, not long for this world.

"My father, Don Angel de la Plata, señores."

He extended a limp hand to Janos. "Señor Janos? I cannot tell you how delighted I was to receive your letter. Delighted. Everything is ready for you. I have had men working at the mine for some weeks now. Some weeks. I am certain you will find things more than satisfactory."

He rambled on in this fashion pausing barely long enough to allow Janos to introduce me and repeated himself constantly, delivering all this in a sharp, querulous old woman's voice that didn't sound healthy at all.

She managed to stop him long enough to make the point that a meal was about to be served in another room. I pushed the wheel chair for her and she led the way out into the hall and through to the rear of the building where a table had been set on a terrace overlooking the overgrown garden.

We were served by two Indian women with dark sullen faces who never said a word, but appeared and disappeared as required.

There was claret in what I can only describe as quantity, tumblers of the stuff, not wineglasses. Each time mine was empty, one of the Indian women filled it again. The food was plain and wholesome and in immense quantities. Typical back country ranch fare. Frijoles with plenty of chile. Fried steaks that were as big as the plate and the finest goat's cheese I have ever tasted. The old man plucked at his food and ate nothing. In fact he even managed to stop speaking, leaving the girl to carry the conversation alone.

"You had a reasonable trip from Huila?" she enquired.

"Quite excellent," Janos told her. "Of course, the automobile makes a great difference. The priest was most impressed, was he not, Keogh?"

"Priest?" she said blankly.

"We found him in Huila trying to arrange transport to Mojada. A Father van Horne, an American. He has been assigned to this parish, I understand. We left him at the church which was, I must say, in a remarkable state."

"Yes, it would be." She was frowning deeply. "Señor, I would like very much to accompany you back to Mojada to speak with this man. Do you mind?"

"Our pleasure, señorita." He coughed. "There is, however, just one slight snag. We were told at the hotel that it would be impossible to accommodate us."

She said calmly, "I will speak to Moreno, the proprietor, there will be no difficulty."

"And when do we get to see the mine, señorita?" I asked.

"I think perhaps in the morning if that would suit you. It is about three miles from here. I would think it impossible for your automobile to negotiate the track, but if you would not mind a buckboard, señor?" she said to Janos.

He bowed slightly. "At your service, señorita. There is just one thing."

"And that is?"

He cleared his throat awkwardly, giving what I had to admit was a most excellent performance. "To be frank with you, señorita, I was approached by the military governor for the area in Huila, a Colonel Bonilla and advised against coming. He seemed to think my associate and I would be in danger of our lives."

"There is no such danger," she said tonelessly. "Colonel Bonilla is not in full possession of the facts."

"Señorita," he said patiently. "You must excuse me for pressing the point, but it was suggested to me that your brother, who is, I understand, unfortunately at odds with the authorities, might interfere in our business."

"I am in charge here, señor, in my father's name." She stood up. "My brother holds no sway here. I will return directly and we can then leave if this is convenient to you."

She went out and I glanced enquiringly at Janos. He shook his head slightly and proceeded to light a cigar.

The old man, who had been sitting in silence for so long, glanced up suddenly, glared malevolently at both of us and shrieked, "Who are you? What are you doing here?"

We both stood up slowly and, behind us, the door opened and Chela de la Plata returned. The old man started to swear monotonously and with considerable obscenity. She held the door wide for us and we walked out.

We left her to it and went out to the Mercedes. As I handed Janos into the rear seat, he said out of the side of his mouth, a fixed smile on his face, "And why didn't Bonilla mention that little item?"

Exactly what I had been thinking myself, but we were prevented from continuing the conversation by the arrival of Chela, still dressed for riding.

She got into the front passenger seat and smiled brightly. "When you are ready, señor."

Just like that without even an attempt at an expla-

nation but as I drove away it was Bonilla I was thinking about and his obviously deliberated omission of
the important point that Don Angel de la Plata was
as mad as a hatter. Now why was that?

EIGHT

Smoke drifted into the late afternoon air in a dense cloud as we approached the village.

"Something seems to be burning," Janos said calmly. "I hope it isn't the church."

Chela de la Plata said in a low, desperate voice, "Hurry, señor, I implore you."

But the church was still standing as we went over the rise and got a clear look at the village below and the smoke seemed to be coming from the other side of the bell tower.

Thirty or forty people were standing in a wide semi-circle, silently watching as we drew up. There was a splintering crash from inside the church and van Horne emerged from the porch. He was stripped to the waist and carried a couple of planks on his shoulder.

"Spring cleaning, Father?" I called as we approached.

He grinned. "Something like that."

I followed him round to the rear of the building and discovered a sizable fire. He hurled the planks into the centre of it and turned.

"I've salvaged what I could. Some of the benches are still intact. What the place will need after this is a damn good scrub and a coat of whitewash."

"You look as if you're enjoying yourself." He ignored the remark and I added quickly, "I'll give you the story on De la Plata later. We've got his daughter with us."

He looked beyond my shoulder and smiled. "Good afternoon, señorita."

When I turned she was standing a short distance away watching. Janos shuffled forward, leaning heavily on his walking stick. "Hot work, Father. Allow me to introduce Señorita de la Plata. Señorita, this is Father van Horne, whom we brought from Huila with us."

Chela de la Plata came forward with a rush, ignoring me completely, directly confronting van Horne. Her face was very white now, the eyes like great dark holes. "You cannot stay here, Father, you must not. They must surely have warned you."

"Of a great many things, señorita." He smiled gently. "My place is here, now, it can be no other way. You must surely realise that."

"They murder priests here, Father," she cried violently. "They will see no reason to treat you differently and I am in this thing. I am involved without wishing to be, have no choice in the matter. And I am tired, Father, tired of the burden of it."

Van Horne responded to the undoubted agony in her voice in a quite astonishing way. He took one of her hands gently in his and smoothed the hair back from her brow with the other. His face was grave, his voice firm and kind.

"This is not on you, child, this business. Not any of it. Do you understand me?"

She gazed up at him in wonderment and then tightened her grip on his hand so much that her knuckles whitened. She closed her eyes momentarily and a great, shuddering sigh slipped from her mouth.

When she opened her eyes again, much of the strain seemed to have left her face. "They will not help you, Father, they have much fear."

"I know."

"Of my brother," she said flatly. "Who hates all things that live."

He smiled and gently disengaged her hand. "Go with God now, señorita. I have work to do. Perhaps when things are more in order here you will come and see me again?"

She walked away back towards the car. I looked at van Horne with a frown, but he ignored me, picked up a plank and put it on the fire. By now he had completely lost me and I turned and went back to the Mercedes. Chela de la Plata ran past me, back to van Horne and I helped Janos into the rear seat of the car and put a foot on the running board.

"What do you think?" I asked him.

"A remarkable performance. I think he almost believed it himself."

"But what if he did, or at least, began to?"

Janos chuckled hoarsely. "By God, sir, that would be ironic."

Something of an understatement, but I was unable to take it further for Chela returned at that precise moment, van Horne at her side.

"I have asked Father van Horne to visit the hacienda tomorrow," she said. "I should like him to meet my father. Perhaps you gentlemen would be good enough to bring him with you?"

"A pleasure to serve you, señorita," Janos said. "This must have been a pleasant little church once."

"Over two hundred years old," she said. "Dedicated

originally to the Blessed Martin de Porres. He was always greatly reverenced in these parts. He had an Indian mother, you know."

"So I believe," I said. "Father van Horne was telling us about him only yesterday. In fact he has a rather interesting image of the saint in his possession."

Van Horne was frowning, for some reason that at the time I did not fully comprehend, although I realise now that he must have seen more than coincidence in the turn events had taken. "This church is dedicated to St. Martin de Porres?"

"But surely you must have known, that, Father?" She appeared to hesitate. "This image you have with you. Could I see it?"

"But of course." He glanced at us, taking her by the arm. "If you gentlemen wouldn't mind waiting?"

They went inside and Janos said, "Now what do you make of that?"

"I know one thing," I told him. "She's well and truly hooked."

"Precisely, which cannot but be to our advantage. He has a way with him, our friend."

"He'll have her confessing to him next."

He paused in the act of slicing the end off a cigar with a small silver penknife. "And this offends you?"

"Shouldn't it?"

"He came here to play a part. You now appear to be jibing at the fact that he's playing it so well."

Which was fair enough and yet the strange, illogical coldness that I felt in the pit of my stomach would not go away, for I had a feeling that events were already taking a completely different course from any considered by us at the beginning of things.

When they emerged into the sunlight again, van

Horne looked serious and grave and Chela de la Plata, very pale. He put a hand on her shoulder and blessed her, then went back inside.

"You found the image pleasing, señorita?" Janos enquired as we drove away.

But she didn't answer him, had not even heard as far as I could judge, and stared straight ahead of her into space, seeing only that which was locked fast in the secret mind of her.

When we reached the hotel, she seemed to have recovered herself and went up the steps briskly, her spurs jangling. Moreno was behind the bar clearing glasses and came round to greet her rather uncertainly, drying his hands on a cloth.

"At your orders, señorita."

"These gentlemen are here on my father's business, Rafael. Two days, perhaps three. Your best rooms will be sufficient."

There was the same look of horror on his face as when he had first seen van Horne. "But señorita," he whispered, "how can I do this thing. It is not permitted."

"Tell me, my friend," she said coldly. "Who owns this place?"

"Why, your father, señorita."

"Then your choice is simple. Either you do as I say or I will have you on the street, bag and baggage. You would like this?"

He fluttered helplessly, a fly in the web. "My wife, as the señorita knows, is in no condition . . ."

"Exactly." There was a ruthless streak in this one a mile wide. "My decision, not yours, Rafael. No harm will come to you."

He collapsed completely. "Very well, señorita, on your head be it."

She turned, a slight, pale smile of triumph on her face. I think that was the first time that it occurred to me that she and her brother must be alike in a great many ways.

We left our baggage for Moreno to take up to the rooms, but didn't bother to inspect them for there was Chela de la Plata to be taken back to the hacienda.

For most of the way, she said absolutely nothing and then, with about half a mile to go, she said suddenly, "You may find the mine rather primitive by your standards, Señor Keogh. It is many years since it was properly worked. I trust you will make allowances."

"As long as there is silver there in economic quantities, señorita, that is the only important thing. Equipment is something we can always bring in."

"Of course." She leaned back in the seat and said, with an abrupt change of course, "Father van Horne is a remarkable man, don't you agree?"

"I'm afraid I don't know him well enough to make that kind of judgement. But he looks the kind of man who could survive most things."

"As do you, señor." She touched the silver amulet around my neck briefly. "A strange thing for a man like you to wear. May I ask where you acquired it?"

"A gift," I said. "From a good friend."

Her eyebrows went up, she seemed to withdraw from me if I can put it so, but in this they were all the same, pure blood or mestizo, they despised the Indian. In some way, I suppose, she looked upon me as contaminated.

"Did I detect a sudden frost?" Janos enquired as I

took the Mercedes back along the track.

I turned, touching the amulet briefly. "My impression is that I've let the side down."

"I'm afraid so," he said. "In Texas or Arizona they would call you squaw man and ride you out of town on a rail, one of the more civilized contributions that great nation has made to Western culture. Would you enjoy living in the Wind River country, Keogh?"

"I can't say, never having been there."

"I have visited the fringes only when I first came to this country. It is not like your Ireland, I assure you. A savage, sterile place. A nightmare landscape of mesas and buttes, lava beds and twisted forests of stone. Life there would be a struggle most days of the week."

"It sounds interesting," I said, humouring him.

"The Apache are known as the enemy of all men," he said. "Yet they fear the Yaqui. For over four hundred years, since Spain first claimed these lands, they have fought the invader and with considerable success, I might add. For many years the government, in despair, attempted a policy of extermination. A cruel and barbaric people, Keogh. They mutilate the bodies of their enemies."

"I've seen men maimed just as effectively with a Mills bomb." I rammed my foot hard down on the brake as a horseman cantered over a rise to the left and reined in his mount in the middle of the road.

I knew who he was instantly for there was no one else it could be. He sat there, slim and erect in the saddle, black jacket and tight-fitting black trousers, not a silver button in sight to relieve his sombre appearance. The face beneath the black sombrero was the face of a ravaged saint, an Anthony burned through to the bone by the heat of the wilderness. The pale blue eyes were quite empty. No love, no cruelty either. Nothing.

THE WRATH OF GOD

He said calmly, "Tomás de la Plata at your orders, gentlemen."

"At yours, señor." Janos gave him back. "My name is . . ."

"I know who you are, just as I know why you are here. This dream of my father's, an old man's foolishness, is this not so?"

On first sight he was not armed, but as he leaned forward slightly, I saw that he carried a revolver in a strap under his left arm.

I said, "How can we know this until we've had a chance of inspecting the mine?"

He nodded slowly and sat there silently staring into space, his face calm as if waiting for something. On the face of it, I would never have a better chance of killing him. He was mine for the taking. Above us on the hill, birds lifted in alarm from the shelter of the cottonwoods.

It had happened once before, just like this, outside a village in County Clare, just after the start of the Civil War. A damned rogue of a tinker leading us in and he playing both sides against the middle. The rooks calling angrily as they drifted up out of the beech trees at the side of the road should have warned me, but by then it was too late and a heavy machine gun cut down every man in the first Crossley tender.

We learn by our mistakes. I said politely, "Your sister has invited us to inspect the mine in the morning, señor."

He said abruptly, "Two days, no more, then you go and I see your report before she does. Do you understand?"

He raised his hand and half-a-dozen riders emerged from the cottonwoods, each man carrying a rifle. They milled around the Mercedes, an unsavoury looking group, mostly dressed like working vaqueros, but all heavily armed.

"This priest you brought with you," Tomás de la Plata said. "He goes back with you when you leave and only because I am in a good humour. Tell him this from me and in the meantime, he approaches the people of Mojada at his peril. No services, no religious propaganda of any kind. I will not have it here."

Janos cleared his throat. "We are not his keepers, señor."

"You would perhaps prefer to be his mourners?" He smiled gently. "There is no choice for this man, señores. There never was. If he stays, he dies."

He put spurs to his horse and galloped away followed by his men. Janos sighed heavily. "For a while there I thought you might try to take him. If you had, we would both have been meat for the crows by now. You knew they were there?"

"They shouldn't have disturbed the birds," I said.

He chuckled. "By God, sir, but you know your business, I can see that."

As I drove away, I could feel the sweat soaking through my shirt and jacket and my hands were trembling.

I left Janos at the Casa Mojada to settle in and strolled through the streets, smoking a cigarette and greeting whoever I saw, although not one single person gave me as much as a good evening in reply.

These were poor people, leading lives as wretched as any lived before the Revolution and their condition made its ideals laughable. Truly, nothing in this life ever did change. What was virtually an open sewer ran down the centre of one street, little children playing listlessly in an atmosphere where the stench of urine and human dirt touched everything.

It ran into a small plaza with a well standing in the centre. An old woman, so old that it seemed a miracle she lived at all, struggled with a stone pitcher of water.

I took it from her, in spite of her protestations and followed her when she turned and fled to one of the hovels opposite. I stooped to enter the door, which gives some indication of its size, considering my modest height, and almost choked on that fetid air. When my eyes grew accustomed to the half-light, I saw that there were no windows and that the only furniture, if you could call it that, was a heap of Indian blankets for bedding in the corner. The old woman crouched fearfully by a smouldering fire. I put the pitcher of water down, pressed a five-peso piece into her hand and left hurriedly.

When I emerged, I saw van Horne standing outside the porch of the church looking down towards me. He was wearing his cassock and clerical collar again.

"Good evening, Father," I called loudly as I got near.

"Mr. Keogh," he turned and led the way into the church. "What have you been doing? Visiting the poor?"

"I wouldn't put a hound-dog I thought anything of into that place," I said. "God knows, I've seen poverty in my time, but the worst slum in Dublin would seem a palace to these people."

"A hard country," he said. "I told you that. Now, what happened at the hacienda?"

I told him everything from the first incident with Jurado to the final confrontation with Tomás de la Plata. When I had finished, he sat on the edge of the vestry table staring into space, a frown on his face.

"Two days," he said at last. "That doesn't give us very long."

"Why do you think Bonilla kept quiet about the old man being crazy? He must have known. Damn, he knows everything else about the family."

He looked at me, frowning slightly. "I get the impression you have your own answer to that one?"

"All right," I said. "If you must know, I think you are more important to this business than Bonilla made clear. I think he intended you to be a stalking horse."

"To draw him in from the mountains where you could get a crack at him?" He shrugged. "That's all right by me, boy. I will kill him myself on the first opportunity, I promise you."

"Then you will disregard the message he sent?"

"I did not come here to take his orders, Keogh. I came to see him under the ground and from what I hear, I'd be performing a public service."

"And what about the woman. What kind of game are you playing there?"

"What game would you have me play?" He was genuinely puzzled. "I'm priest here, boy, and priest I must be. Does that offend you in some way? I had got the impression that religious belief was hardly a strong point with you."

"It isn't," I said. "You seemed to be someone else again, that's all."

"You'll have to take that further. I don't follow you."

"For God's sake, man. I accepted you for a priest myself watching you with her. The way you spoke and acted. Don't take yourself too seriously, that's all."

I walked out of the vestry into the church, my knees shaking for some reason and he followed me, catching me by the arm, turning me easily with that enormous strength of his.

"I'm a murderer, Keogh, and a thief many times over. God doesn't exist for a man like me. He can't."

"If that's true," I said, "if he doesn't exist, then why do the things you've done bother you so much?"

It was the one and only time I got through to the heart of him. His face, or the mask that was his face, melted away and underneath was a man in torment if ever I have seen one. He reached out and grabbed for the front of my coat. I have never known such pure, elemental strength. He had me off the ground like a rubber ball and I thought my final hour had come. And then, abruptly, he seemed to be shaken with some kind of spasm and released me.

"And what about you?" he said. "A man who lives for nothing, believes in nothing, not even himself any more. No emotion left in you. Neither love, nor hate. A dead man walking, Keogh."

He turned, went into the vestry and closed the door and I stood there, filled with a kind of horror, for in describing me, he had duplicated, almost word for word, my own impression of Tomás de la Plata.

I started to turn away and paused, the breath catching in my throat. The obscene chalk drawing on the front of the altar had been washed away and on top stood a small wooden crucifix, another of the items from the trunk. The figure of Christ was in silver and a final dying ray of the evening sun reached in through the narrow window to touch it brightly.

I turned and fled as if all the hounds in heaven were snapping at my heels.

The rooms at the hotel were as Spartan as I had expected with the whitewashed walls, old brass beds and furniture that looked as if it had been made locally and not by an expert.

I found Janos sitting by the side of his bed at the open window. He had a cloth spread across his knees and was engaged in cleaning his revolver, a Smith & Wesson .38.

"Did you see van Horne?" he asked me.

I nodded. "Yes, I saw him."

"And quarrelled from the sound of you."

"Something like that, but it isn't important. I looked in the mirror for a moment and didn't care for what was there."

"A pointless exercise, my friend, as I discovered long ago. Let's see if we can get some food out of our reluctant host and perhaps a drink or two. You'll feel better for it."

Reluctant Moreno certainly was although he certainly saw that we were fed in a private room at the back and served by his wife who was obviously having trouble in hauling herself around with that great swollen belly of hers. I felt like telling him so forcibly, but then it was hardly my affair and this was a land where women, at least in the back country, were beasts of burden from the day they were born.

I watched her drag herself out at the end of the meal and Janos said, "She doesn't look too healthy."

"An understatement," I said. "If she carries on like that, she'll be in real trouble."

"But of course," he said. "I was forgetting. You had medical training. But never qualified?"

"A year to go."

"Which seems a pity. Have you ever considered going back to complete the course?"

"To Dublin?" I laughed shortly. "I'd get short shrift

there, believe me. Let's try the bar and see what he's got to offer."

Which was as good a way of cutting off the conversation as any as I think he knew. A wise old bird, there was no doubt about that.

Moreno was not in the bar when we went in, which was fortunate in a way for when I went behind to help myself, I discovered a stock of scotch whisky of excellent quality. I could guess who it was kept for, but helped myself to a bottle anyway and two glasses. Moreno came in at that moment and seemed about to protest but thought better of it.

"Is there anything else you require, señores?"

"A pack of cards, I think, or perhaps even two. Janos looked at me hopefully. "You don't play bezique, by any chance?"

"No, but I once spent two months with my leg up in a Connemara farmhouse with an English general we were holding hostage who taught me a diabolical little game called piquet."

An expression of complete and utter delight suffused his face. "My God, sir, but I never thought to see the day again when I could play a gentleman's game."

He gave me a cigar and while we were lighting them, Moreno returned with the cards. He put them on the table and said diffidently, "Perhaps the señores would be more comfortable in a private room. It gets a little crowded in here later on."

"We're perfectly happy where we are, man," Janos snapped, his hands already busy with the pack, discarding all the cards below seven. "Now leave us in peace."

I should have known how good he would be, but

even being rubiconed by Janos was an enjoyable experience. It took my mind off things admirably to such
an extent that when we paused after the first hour, I
was surprised to find a dozen or fifteen other custo-
mers in the place.

We were intruders, so much was obvious and mostly
they sat in silence, watching us sullenly while they
drank or muttered together in low voices. They were
all local men, simple peons from their dress and certainly nothing to worry about.

We started on a fresh game and I was on the third
deal of the *partie* when the door opened and Raul Jurado entered, spurs jingling. There were two other
men with him, dressed like him as vaqueros, pistols at
their belts and one of them had been with Tomás de la
Plata when last I saw him.

Jurado scowled heavily and stood glaring at us for a
moment, a leather quirt dangling from his left wrist.
He would have dearly loved to throw us out or worse,
but that course of action was denied him now on the
word of the man who was obviously his true master.

He moved to the bar and ordered tequila for himself and his friends from Moreno who looked absolutely terrified. A moment later the door opened again and
Oliver van Horne stepped inside.

There was complete and utter silence of a quite remarkable kind and the astonishment on the faces of
everyone there was something to see.

Van Horne said pleasantly, "Good evening."

"And a good evening to you, Father." I was the only
one to speak.

He was wearing his cassock and shovel hat and carried a bundle under his arm wrapped in a woollen

blanket. He went over to the bar and addressed Moreno.

"Señor, I'm sorry to bother you but I'm in urgent need of one or two items and thought you might be able to assist."

Moreno stared at him, petrified, and Jurado turned to watch, an ugly glint in his eye.

"A mattress for my bed," van Horne continued in the same calm voice. "An oil lamp and as much whitewash as you can spare and the brushes to apply it."

"There is nothing for you here," Jurado said. "Go away."

Van Horne said mildly, "I am a poor man and unable to pay in cash until my funds come through, but it occurred to me that you might be willing to hold this as security."

He unwrapped the blanket and set the image of St. Martin de Porres on the bar counter. There was a startled gasp, more than one, a chair went over with a crash as someone rose involuntarily. Two men went down on their knees and most there crossed themselves.

"Merciful heaven," Moreno said and there was awe on his face. "But where did you find him, Father?"

"You recognise it?"

"Ah, yes." Moreno crossed himself with as much devotion as any man could. "He belongs here, Father, here in our own church where he stood in the side chapel from the day the church was built. For two hundred years. He is ours, Father, he belongs to the people of this place. When he was taken during the Revolution, he took our luck with him."

"He will be yours again, my friend," van Horne told him. "Back in his place in the chapel once the church has been cleaned and re-consecrated."

"I will get you the things you need now, Father," Moreno said, "if you will come this way."

Jurado's quirt lashed down across the bar counter. "And I say no!"

Van Horne faced him. "By what authority?"

"Will this do, señor priest?"

Jurado pulled out his pistol, extended his arm and shoved the muzzle into van Horne's belly.

I had my hand inside my coat ready to draw, but there was no need. Van Horne calmly pushed the barrel of the pistol to one side. "Hardly a contest, señor, when I am not armed. I had thought you a man of honour."

Jurado was stupid enough to fall for it. He glared at van Horne, looked around the room as if to assert his authority and holstered his pistol. "You are proposing some kind of contest?"

"Why not?" van Horne said. "A little harmless amusement and no harm done. A trial of strength. If I win, you allow Moreno to give me what I need."

"And if you lose?"

Van Horne shrugged. "That will be up to you, señor."

Jurado laughed, and struck his nearest companion in the chest sending him half across the room. "Trial of strength—with me? That's funny, isn't it? That's the funniest thing I ever heard." He turned back to van Horne. "What do you propose?"

"Indian wrestling," van Horne said.

Jurado's mouth gaped. "Indian wrestling? A game for children."

He looked angry, suspecting he was being played with. Van Horne said, "I have a variation which adds a little interest. Let me show you."

There were several candles burning in holders on

the top shelf behind the bar. He asked Moreno for two of them, took them to the nearest table and positioned them carefully. I saw the purpose of this at once as did most others watching. In Indian wrestling the antagonists sit opposite each other, right hands clasped, elbows on the table and the object is to force the opponent's hand down on to the table. Van Horne's variation meant a nasty burn for the loser into the bargain.

Jurado laughed and grabbed a chair. "Heh, I like this. I like this very much indeed, though I warn you, señor, I may forget to let go."

Van Horne sat opposite him, they placed their elbows on the table and clasped hands. Jurado was grinning, teeth bared, but I could not see van Horne's face for his back was towards me.

A muscle ridged in Jurado's face, his smile was a little tighter now as he realised he had taken on more than he had bargained for. Van Horne's arm started to go, slowly, but surely, down towards the candle flame.

The triumph on Jurado's face was there for all to see. He laughed out loud and then his smile slipped completely as his hand was forced upwards again, straight over the top and down to the other candle in a single smooth motion that told us all that van Horne had been playing with him.

He held the hand against the flame and Jurado's face twisted in agony, sweat standing out on his forehead in great drops and yet he would not cry out, teeth clenched and in the end, van Horne released him and stood up.

"A great French king once said, let any man who says he has not known fear try snuffing out a candle flame between his finger and thumb. Of course it all depends on how you do it."

He licked his finger and thumb and nipped both

candles quickly. Jurado stood staring at him, pain on his face, nursing his injured hand, then turned and stamped out, followed by his two friends.

Van Horne picked up the image of St. Martin de Porres, wrapped it carefully during the silence that followed and went out through the door which Moreno held open for him.

Conversation burst through to the surface with a vengeance after that. I leaned forward and said to Janos, "What in the hell was he up to?"

"God alone knows, but he'll need a gun next time." He gathered up the cards. "Enough excitement for one night. I'm for bed."

I watched him go, then got to my feet and moved out to the porch. There were two or three men sitting there who fell silent at my approach. As I moved to the edge of the step, there was the rattle of wheels over the cobbles and a handcart came round from the rear of the building pushed by Moreno. Van Horne walked at his side.

I went down the steps and called to him. He paused, then told Moreno to continue. "What do you want?"

I said, "What were you supposed to be playing at in there?"

"Establishing my authority, that's all. When the woman recognised the image this morning and told me its history, I knew at once that I was on to a good thing, but it had to be exploited. I think I've managed that very satisfactorily, don't you? I'll see you in the morning."

He walked away into the darkness after the handcart and I stood there listening to him go, wondering again which one of him was the real Oliver van Horne, but that was a puzzle to which I might never get an answer.

I felt restless and ill-at-ease, certainly in no mood for sleep. I went down through the main street, such as it was, aware of the foul stench of the open drain and moved quickly to the main gate in the wall. Outside, the air was fresh and sweet, stars strung away to the horizon, snow on the high peaks glittering in the moonlight.

Higher up the slopes in the cottonwoods by the stream, a fire glimmered in the night in the centre of a small encampment and horses and mules grazed peacefully, hobbled for the night. I heard the faint tinkle of an ornamental bell round one animal's neck, gentle on the night breeze and the heart in me seemed to stop beating.

I passed one guard and then another and neither challenged me. One man slept beside the fire rolled in a blanket. Nachita sat cross-legged on the other side smoking a pipe, his Winchester across his knees.

His face seemed ageless in the flickering firelight as he looked across at me, but not as timeless as hers when she raised the tent flap and stood watching me calmly. As old as time, every woman who had ever lived rolled into one and in that moment I could understand those people in other days who had worshipped a goddess instead of a god.

She smiled and that smile was for me alone and I went past her into the tent. A storm lamp hung from the ridge pole and she pulled down the flap, closing out the world and dropped to her knees.

I squatted in front of her, watching as she unbraided her hair expertly until it hung in a dark curtain below her shoulders. Then she did a thing which surprised me. She opened a flat wooden box, took out a pad of writing paper and a pencil and wrote something quickly.

It was in Spanish, of course, and in excellent handwriting. It said quite simply: "Did you think I could ever leave you?"

A difficult thing to answer, but there was no need for she stood up and blew out the light.

NINE

For years I had lived a life in which everything had, of necessity, to be sacrificed to the Cause. There had been no room for honour, friendship, love or any kind of human response that might be considered a weakness.

I was not used to involvement and the responsibilities that came with it. I was a solitary, lonely man and content to be so and mainly because of the fact that for so many years I had not expected to live beyond the day after tomorrow.

But now there was Victoria, had been from that first moment at Tacho's when she had run to my side, clutching at my jacket like a lost child recognising a loved one in a crowd.

She is in your care now, señor. Tacho's words came back to haunt me, but I was beginning to wonder if it wasn't the other way round. She had changed considerably since choosing sides. Had become all Yaqui. Van Horne had once said that she would take a knife to me in bed the first time I displeased her. Most likely on last night's performance, that she would take a knife to anyone who harmed me.

So, she was wholly in my mind as I drove the Mercedes out through the gate on the following morning, van Horne beside me and Janos in the rear as usual and when I saw the encampment still there by the stream, smoke rising from the fire, I was filled with a feeling of real and conscious pleasure.

She was standing by the fire, leaning over a cooking pot. Nachita spoke to her and she glanced up, shading her eyes from the morning sun. Then she did a strange thing. She ran across to the nearest horse, swung up on its bare back and urged it into a gallop.

There was only the rope halter to hang on to, but she was a marvellous rider and was beside us in a moment, her face turned towards me. She was laughing, perhaps at the very joy of living on such a morning although I like to think it was because of me. I waved and as we drew away, she pulled her mount round and went back towards the camp.

Van Horne said, "I told you she wouldn't let go, Keogh."

"Did I ever say I wanted her to?"

He seemed surprised, but said simply, "You go to hell in your own way, boy."

"Exactly," Janos said patiently. "Could we now discuss the day's plan of campaign?"

"Simplicity itself," van Horne said. "I came here to get De la Plata one way or the other as Bonilla suggested, not to commit suicide."

"I could have taken him yesterday," I said. "And been dead meat after, his men would have seen to that."

"Exactly, so we have to draw him into some kind of direct confrontation, either alone or with the kind of backing we can take care of."

"And how do we manage that?"

"We play it by ear and hope. I suggest you make your inspection of the mine this morning, then tell the girl and the old man you'll consider all the relevant

facts, compile a report on the situation this afternoon. She'll ask you back for a meeting to discuss
things this evening, nothing is more certain."

"And you think Tomás will put in an appearance?"
Janos asked.

"There or at the hotel. He'll want to know what's
in that report. Wouldn't you agree, Keogh?"

I nodded slowly. "I'd be surprised if he didn't. The
thing is, will he turn up on his own?"

"We'll just have to wait and see, won't we?"

He lit a cigarillo, leaned back cheerfully, took a
book from his pocket and started to read. It was a
copy of St. Augustine's *City of God* in Latin, but I had
ceased to be surprised at anything now where van
Horne was concerned.

As we drove into the courtyard and came to a halt at
the bottom of the steps, Chela de la Plata appeared in
the doorway. She was dressed for riding as she had
been the previous day in leathern breeches and boots,
the Cordoban hat tilted over her eyes. The riding
whip in her left hand tapped nervously against her leg
and she seemed tired and drawn, the pale skin
stretched tightly over the cheekbones.

She came down to meet us, a manilla folder in one
hand bound with red tape which she handed to me.
"You will find assay reports in there for the last five
years the mine was fully operating and other information which I presume you will need."

Janos removed his hat. "May I enquire how your
father is this morning?"

"Not well, I'm afraid. He is confined to his bed." She
hesitated, then turned to van Horne. "He is in no condition to see visitors, Father. I am sorry to have wasted
your time in this manner."

"I understand perfectly," he told her, and for a moment, there was that strange quality of intimacy between them that I had noticed during their first meeting at the church.

She brightened suddenly. "Perhaps you would care to accompany us to the mine? Many of the village men are working there at the moment. You might find it of interest."

"I'd like nothing better."

"You ride, Father?"

"I've been known to."

She smiled in a way she hadn't smiled in a long, long time unless I was mistaken. Strange, but they had talked together as if Janos and I had ceased to exist.

The trail was difficult, mainly because of the kind of terrain it had to cross, but it had also deteriorated due to neglect over the years. It was obviously the first matter that would require attention if the mine was ever to become fully operational again.

Van Horne and I followed Chela in single file, allowing our mounts to pick their own way and Janos toiled along behind in a buckboard hauled by two horses, one of the hacienda's peons at the reins.

We ascended into a country of broken hills and narrow, twisting water courses. The slopes were covered with mesquite and greasewood and as we climbed higher, a few *piñones* rooted in the scant soil, pushing their pointed heads into the morning.

We went over a rise to a small plateau and found half-a-dozen men ranged across the path, each with his reins in his left hand, his rifle in the right. All very military, but as I remembered, Tomás de la Plata had been an army officer.

He appeared from the *piñones* above us, a sombre, rather clerical-looking figure in his black clothes. Chela was angry and frightened at the same time.

"What is it?" she called. "What do you want? You gave me your word. You promised two days."

One of his men urged his horse in close, reached inside my coat and plucked the Enfield from my shoulder holster, had obviously been told beforehand exactly where to look.

"Tomás!" Chela cried, a kind of agony in her voice.

"I gave my word," he said. "Now carry on to the mine. Your friends will follow when I have finished with them."

She knew him, I suppose, well enough to know the futility of arguing, but her face was white and angry as she hauled her mount round viciously and rode away.

The buckboard was still some considerable way down the trail behind us and Janos was well out of things. Tomás pushed his hat back to hang round his neck and stood looking down at us for a while. He had pale flaxen hair, strange for a Mexican, blue eyes and the aesthetic face was calm, empty. Yes, empty was an excellent word to describe it.

"Come up here, Señor Keogh," he said, "and bring the priest with you."

We did as we were told, not that we had any option in the matter, dismounted and scrambled up the bank to find him leaning against a tree smoking a cigarette.

He behaved at first as if van Horne didn't exist. "When will you be ready with an opinion on the mine?"

"I'm not sure," I said. "I'll have to look at the place this morning, go through the figures your sister has given me this afternoon, then prepare a report."

"You have arranged to see her and my father this evening?"

"No, I understand he's not too well. He's confined to his bed."

"I wish to see this report when it is finished, you understand me?"

"I would have thought that your sister's business under present circumstances, not yours," van Horne told him quietly.

Tomás de la Plata said in a voice of dreadful calm, "I was not aware that I had given you permission to speak, but now I have started, let me make one thing clear. I allow you to survive at my sister's urging for two days only and in that time, no preaching, no approaches to the people, no priest's tricks. Two days, then you go. If you break my conditions in the meantime, I shall kill you."

"And that would give you some kind of pleasure?" van Horne said.

"No more than to put my foot on a beetle." He turned and looked at me speculatively. "You saw Colonel Bonilla in Huila. He warned you against coming here?"

"That's right."

"And what did he tell you about me?"

"He said that the people had had their Revolution. That what they and the country needs now is stability and order, which means there can be no room for men like you."

Why I had said it and in quite that way, I do not know, but the words were out and impossible to retrieve. It didn't seem to matter for only one aspect of what I had said registered with him.

He turned to look at me and his eyes seemed to have

changed colour, glittering like pieces of ice in the pale face. "The people," he said. "You speak to me of the people? Shall I tell you what they are? Dung on the face of the land. I went to prison for them, spent three years in a penal colony for political offenders in the jungles of Yucatán. Suffered every conceivable degradation. I gave my life to a struggle whose one ideal was to win them their freedom and freedom they took. To murder, to rape and burn and turn this land into a charnel house."

"They were under the boot for a considerable time," I reminded him. "A reaction that might have been expected."

"You think so?" He shivered as if suddenly cold and stared out over the mountainside and it was as if he was speaking to himself. "Not by me, señor. I came home after ten years of fighting the people's war to find my father a broken old man more out of his wits than in them, a sister who cried out in terror if a man even brushed her sleeve in passing."

There was a stillness, only the slightest of breezes through the *piñones* and for a moment, it was so quiet that I could hear the wheels of the buckboard on the hillside below.

"They came to my home one night in the last months of the war, soldiers of the ranks of the Revolution and their commanding officer, an animal named Varga, military governor in the area. My father, they beat half to death, left him for dead after defecating on his body as he lay there. As for my sister, Varga took her for himself, abused and degraded her in every possible way, then gave her to the men."

The story was such a commonplace one, that was the dreadful thing, for I could have capped it with accounts of a score such incidents known to me, the details of which were even more horrifying.

It was van Horne who spoke then, his voice harsh and angry. "And no one did anything to prevent this? No one stood by them?"

"The people of Mojada stayed home like whipped dogs and the priest of that time, their spiritual adviser, had room in his life for only two things each day. At least one full bottle of tequila and the stinking bed of the widow who kept house for him. A father to his people as you can see."

"And for this you became the enemy of all the world?"

"Once I believed in reason and the intellect, señor, but I learned better. I learned the true worth of men. I cut Varga's throat with my own hand, hung the priest and the one who came after him and as for the people? They would eat their own dirt if I ordered it."

"And this makes you a happy man?" van Horne asked.

Tomás de la Plata glared at him and the eyes seemed to enlarge, grew darker. When he extended two fingers of his left hand, that hand was shaking. "Two days, priest. Two days." He turned and in the same breath added, "And you, señor, will be hearing from me at the appropriate time. Now go."

As we scrambled down the bank his men urged their horses up to join him. There was a brief flurry and they were away through the *piñones*. The Enfield was lying on top of a boulder. I picked it up carefully, checked the loading and pushed it into the shoulder holster.

Van Horne's face was grey. He said, "I don't know about you, but he scared the hell out of me. He's over the edge, that one."

"And beyond," I said.

The buckboard came over the rise below us and rolled to a halt. Janos called, "I thought you'd be there by now. What happened? Did you run into trouble?"

"Oh, I think you could say that," I told him and van Horne started to laugh, but it was flat, cold stuff, no mirth in it at all.

Our final destination proved to be a small plateau against the great rocky face of the mountain. Chela de la Plata had ridden down to meet us, reining in her horse beside van Horne who led the way.

I didn't hear what she said, but he reached out to take her hand and smiled confidently. "Everything is fine, I promise. He has no intention of breaking his word."

The relief in her face was there for all to see and she pulled ahead to lead the way up on to the plateau, reined in and dismounted. It was a drift mine, the entrance, a large irregular hole in the cliff face and nearby an old steam engine, obviously the major source of power, puffed smoke into the still air.

Water had been channelled down the face of the mountain in several places, running finally into a wooden conduit that emptied into a large dilapidated shed, open at both ends and used to process the ore.

It was a scene of great activity. Periodically, a truck laden with ore emerged from the mouth of the mine pushed by a couple of sweating peons stripped to the waist. The rusting rails took this down a short incline into the ore shed where the processing took place.

Inside the shed, the only piece of machinery was a steam operated crusher and the heat from its furnace made working conditions almost unbearable. The water ran into a tank lined with clay against leakage, and there were the usual cradles and puddling troughs. Perhaps half-a-dozen men worked in there, all stripped to the waist and a young boy spent his time dousing them with buckets of water when called upon to do so.

"As you can see," Chela said, "our methods are primitive by the standards you gentlemen are used to."

"Which can be remedied easily enough," Janos told her. "As long as the prospect exists for the right kind of return, then the introduction of modern machinery and methods will be our first priority."

"Since starting again, what particular problems have you had?" I asked her.

"So many rockfalls that I have lost count."

"Then your timbering must be at fault," Janos said. "Only to be expected after so many years of idleness and decay. Have you any kind of expert assistance available?"

"Many of the villagers worked here before when the mine was fully operational. Rafael Moreno from the hotel was shift foreman as a young man and also an expert shot-firer. He is supervising the work at the rock face for us and Jurado organises the actual labour force."

On her brother's insistence, presumably, but Janos let it go and smiled brightly. "Señorita, I have a confession to make. I have had a hatred of confined places since childhood. Surprising, I know, in one with my business interests. That is why I employ professionals such as Mr. Keogh to give me the benefit of their expert advice."

"Which means you'll sit out here enjoying a cigar while I do the necessary tour of inspection," I said.

"Correct." He smiled rather complacently and perfectly in character. "The privilege not only of age, but of position, Mr. Keogh. I shall sit on a boulder in the sun contemplating this extraordinary view and think of you down there in the darkness—often."

Chela de la Plata smiled. "Then if I may be your guide, Señor Keogh and yours, Father?"

And so the three of us left him in the sunlight and ventured into the darkness.

At the Hermosa Mine there had been considerable criminal element provided by the local state prison and the rest of the labour force had consisted of men newly released from the ranks of the army of the Revolution. A pot constantly on the boil.

The company had operated according to the age-old formula of working them until they dropped, but one essential requirement always faced up to was the need for adequate ventilation for underground, you either breathed or died. A step inside the tunnel and the heat seized me by the throat, which gave me an opportunity to play mining engineer.

"What's wrong with the ventilation?"

"The main airshaft was blocked by a rockfall a week or two back. Moreno says it would take quite an operation to clear it so we decided to carry on for the time being."

"Surely he told you how dangerous that could be?"

"We are short of everything, señor, time as well as money and we needed as much ore out as possible to be in a position to raise more capital. A vicious circle."

We turned a corner and the light faded, leaving us in a corridor of shadows, patches of light illuminated by guttering candles in niches in the rock, marching into the darkness at spaced intervals. We stood to one side as a truck rattled over the rails pushed by a couple of weary, dust-covered men who seemed at the end of their tether.

"As you can see, the work takes a great deal out of them. They can only manage an hour or two at a time in the heat and are then compelled to return to the surface."

"Which would all be effectively remedied by a reasonable ventilating system, I presume, as Mr. Keogh indicates," van Horne said helpfully.

We reached a fork and Chela paused. "There are two main faces. Have you any preference?"

"I think I'd like a chance to speak to Moreno," I said.

"Then we must try what we call Old Woman. He is usually there."

There was a lamp on a hook in the wall. She took it down and led the way, stooping as the tunnel closed in. There was a strange, humming vibration in the rock, sure sign that picks were at work not too far away, a light in the distance, and we emerged into a low-roofed cavern illuminated by a couple of pressure lamps.

A dozen or fifteen men worked at the rock face, jabbing away with short-handled picks. Three or four more gathered ore into baskets which they then emptied into another truck. It was almost impossible to breathe because of the heat and the dust. One of the men at the face got up and came to meet us and in spite of the sweatband around his forehead, the patina of dust, I recognised Moreno.

"Señorita." He nodded his head awkwardly.

"You will answer any questions Señor Keogh puts to you," she told him.

He turned to me, obviously uncertain. There was a sudden shower of soil and pebbles in the corner and one of the men got out of the path fast.

"The timbering could be better," I said.

He took out a knife, sprung the blade and jabbed at the nearest prop, breaking away a large, brittle flake. "As you can see, the wood is old, dried-out to the point of desiccation. The whole mountain waits to come down on us. Each time a man coughs another rock falls."

"Which is why you aren't using machinery down here?"

"The vibration might be all that is needed."

I asked him one or two more reasonably intelligent questions about ore samples and so on, then we left and went back along the tunnel until we reached the place where it forked.

"Would you like to see the other face?" she asked me. "The one we call Crazy Man?"

It was necessary, I suppose to make things look as authentic as possible although the sooner I was out of the place, the happier I would be.

I said, "A brief visit only, señorita, I promise you."

She turned to van Horne. "The tunnel to Crazy Man drops to four feet in places. An uncomfortable journey for you particularly and not necessary."

"Then I'll wait for you here," he told her.

I didn't blame him for his enormous size was ill-suited to the conditions we had found and he had scraped his head on roof trusses more than once on our way to the other face.

We left him there and started along the tunnel, which was in many ways a replica of the first except for the fact that the roof came down to meet us rather sooner than I had expected, in spite of her warning. I was aware of the same vibration in the rock, the tapping of picks. We got out of the way of another truck which scraped past us, its top almost touching the roof. When it had gone, we moved on towards the dim light at the far end.

There was a considerable amount of angry shouting, disagreeably loud in that confined space and when we finally emerged into the cavern which contained the working face, I quickly discovered the cause—Jurado, his face a mask of dust and sweat, a rawhide whip in one hand.

He cracked it at the heels of the men who loaded the baskets with ore. "Come on you lazy scum. Faster!"

Like van Horne, the man had not been built for such work and his enormous bulk obviously made his existence in such a place extremely uncomfortable. The anger and frustration showed clearly in the eyes, the twitching whip and his face and chest were thick with dust.

He nodded to Chela, ignoring me completely. She said, "Is there anything you wish to know, Señor Keogh?"

"I don't think so," I replied. "Conditions here seem much the same as at Old Woman."

She turned to Jurado. "Everything is in order?"

"It would be if these miserable swine would put their backs into it."

"Surely the fault of their working conditions?" I said. "I would have thought the whip possessed only a limited application."

"You don't know these people as I do. It is all they understand."

One of the men collecting ore hoisted his basket to the edge of the truck, paused to take breath and lost his grip, tipping the contents over the floor. Jurado sprang forward and started to belabour him with the weighted handle of the whip.

Chela de la Plata grabbed his arm and cried, "Leave him, Jurado, I order you."

His control had gone to such a degree that he lashed out, catching her across the side of the face with his clenched fist, sending her back into my arms. In the same moment, the unfortunate peon who had been the cause of things tried to make a run for it. Jurado lunged at him, lost his footing and fell against one of the timber roof supports, his great weight knocking it from position.

A waterfall of shale and pebbles erupted from the darkness above. The men who had been working at the face were on their feet with cries of alarm, already moving towards the tunnel and already too late.

There was a distinct cracking sound as a twenty-foot roof truss split in the centre and the mountain rushed in on us.

The air had changed into layers of thick whirling dust that was impossible to breathe. I found myself on my back. The most frightening discovery of all was to find that my legs were trapped and yet, at the first frantic kick, they pulled free of what turned out to be nothing more than a great mound of earth and shale.

I groped forward blindly through the curtain of dust towards a dim glow on the floor and found the pressure lamp half buried. I pumped it up quickly to increase the brightness and held it above my head.

Chela crouched on her hands and knees, dazed and frightened, a streak of blood on her cheek staining the dust and on a first quick check, most of the miners seemed to be in one piece.

Jurado was standing against the rock face, a look of complete incomprehension on his face. It was as if he could not believe that this was happening to him. As

I held up the lamp, illuminating the working and its furthest corners, he gave an angry growl and scrambled up the sloping ramp of rubble which now blocked the entrance to the tunnel.

He started to tear at the top of the mound with his bare hands and several of the miners joined him, coughing spasmodically as they choked on the thick dust. Chela got to her feet and stood there, swaying a little as if uncertain of her balance. I put out a hand to steady her and she pulled away from me violently. So, even in circumstances like this she could not help but react on being touched by a man as her brother had described, but before I could do or say anything, there was a hoarse cry from Jurado.

When I scrambled up beside him with the lamp, I saw that there was now a distinct gap between the heap of rubble and the roof of the tunnel and there was a steady current of air moving through. It was all that was needed. The men started working like beavers and I went back to Chela and took her firmly by the arm.

She started to react in the same violent manner, trying to pull free of me. I slapped her face and shook her hard. "Will you damn well listen to me? It's going to be all right. We're going to get out."

She stopped struggling, staring at me rather vacantly as if unable to comprehend, and the mountain chose that moment to deposit another couple of tons of rubble in the far corner. She came into my arms and held on tight.

Not too long after that, Jurado called to me again. I sat her down against the rock face, climbed up the sloping pile of rubble to join the others. There was a gap a good foot wide now, light streaming through from the other side, voices.

It was with no particular surprise that I saw Oliver van Horne peering through at me.

It took perhaps an hour of hard work from both sides to create a gap on top of the rockfall about ten feet long and two high, just right for a cautious passage out, and not before time for the mountain groaned above our heads and the roof trusses moved uneasily as if in protest at having to continue to carry all that weight.

Chela was second out and only because Jurado went through the instant the passage was clear in what can only be described as indecent haste. I brought up the rear and found Moreno waiting on the other side with two or three men to help me through.

"Father van Horne has gone on ahead with the señorita," he told me. "She seemed much disturbed."

A remark which certainly ranked as the understatement of the day, but I was concerned with only one thing at that moment, which was getting to some fresh air. When I finally stumbled out into the sunlight, everyone was there, not only the workers, but also Tomás de la Plata and his men.

He had Chela on the ground against his knee, one arm about her shoulders as he gently wiped the filth from her face with a damp cloth provided by one of his men who stood holding a bucket of water. As I discovered later, he had been attracted by the sound of the alarm bell which hung in a tripod by the ore shed and was always rung in time of disaster.

Van Horne watched, stripped to the waist, exhibiting the kind of muscular development that would not have disgraced a heavyweight wrestler. Jurado, the cause of it all, stood hesitantly by, wild-eyed.

Tomás de la Plata looked up as I appeared, his face

white and angry. "So, now you know how things stand here, Señor Keogh and no need of any official reports. I will hear no more of this nonsense which has almost cost me my sister's life."

Interesting that the emphasis should be upon his own loss and not hers. If there was a time to throw Jurado to the wolves it was then, but to my surprise, Chela opened her eyes and said simply, "Take me home, Tomás."

He murmured something softly that was for no one but her, kissed her on the brow, then picked her up in his arms. When he went, he took her on the saddle before him, his men following behind and all watched them go in silence.

It was Janos who spoke first and the remark was typical. "By God, sir, Mr. Keogh, but you have a remarkable facility for survival in all things."

"It can't come any closer than that. The roof was still coming down as we got out." I managed a weary grin for van Horne. "A beautiful sight, that face of yours peering through."

I walked to a nearby water trough, sluiced my head and shoulders, then slumped down on the ground, my face turned to the sun. It was too good to last, of course, for Moreno, who had been moving amongst the men making a tally, came and stood before me, his face grave.

"We are missing one man, señor."

I got up wearily and van Horne, who was washing himself at the trough, turned at once.

"Are you certain?"

"Oh yes, señor, José Jardona, the shot-firer on that face. There can be no question."

Jurado, who had been sitting sullenly on the ground, his back against one wall of the ore shed, got to his feet and came forward. "He will be dead by now."

"We can't be certain," I said. "We'll have to go and see."

"Don't be a fool," he said. "How long were we in there before getting out? An hour at least. Did anyone hear a sound?" He turned in appeal to the miners who stood listening in a semi-circle. No one answered and he turned back to me. "He must have been killed instantly under that first fall."

I said to Moreno, "You'll come with me?"

There was fear on his face, real fear and he was, after all, no longer young. He took a deep breath and gave me a queer little bow. "At your orders, señor, but no one else, not under the circumstances."

Hardly a pleasant thought, but it made sense. He started towards the mine and Jurado caught me by the shoulder. "Don't be a fool, the mountain still moves."

But he was more afraid for himself than me and I pulled away and went after Moreno. When I joined him, he already had two pressure lamps burning, gave me one and we started in.

Van Horne caught up with us just as we reached the fork in the tunnel.

Crawling back across the rockfall, the roof of the tunnel close enough to occasionally scrape my back, was not the most rewarding of experiences, especially as the rattle of falling stones and soil could be heard monotonously in the darkness ahead.

When I went back inside the working, it was to find a scene of even greater chaos. There had obviously been a bad fall quite recently and the mountain, squeezing in, had reduced the size of things by half, roof trusses and props smashed like matchsticks and pointing every which-way.

Just to move amongst them was a hazard and yet it was not to be avoided for a low, continuous moaning, as of someone in great pain, led us to the corner where the full force of the first fall had been felt.

Jardona was under a ton or so of rock, his head and shoulders and one arm only clear, the dust-covered face glistening with sweat. I can only presume that he had lost his senses at the first shock and had lain unconscious in the darkness of the corner during the time we had been clearing our way out.

Moreno started to dig carefully with his hands, feeling his way gingerly. After a while he looked at me and shook his head slightly. Not that it mattered for José Jardona was a dying man, had only clung to life this long by a miracle.

He opened his eyes and stared blankly at us and then something clicked, a kind of wonder. His lips moved and he said quite distinctly, "Father, is it you?"

I found van Horne at my shoulder. He was stripped to the waist again, the face a mask of dust. He ran the back of a hand across his eyes as if to clear them and edged forward.

"I saw you at the church," Jardona said. "There was a fire." He closed his eyes again, shuddering in pain, then opened them and said weakly, "I am going to die, Father, and I've done so many terrible things. I didn't think it would matter, but it does."

There was a sudden rumble like distant thunder above us and I ducked, arms raised to cover my head as shale and rubble cascaded across us.

There was blood on Jardona's mouth. He spat it out and said weakly, "Don't leave me, Father."

Van Horne took his hand and a roof truss cracked and sagged in the far corner. He glanced over his

THE WRATH OF GOD

shoulder and said, "No sense in you two staying."

Moreno, poor devil, looked as if he expected to meet his Maker at any moment and yet some stubborn streak would not allow him to betray his manhood. "José is my cousin, señor." He smiled apologetically. "A matter of family, you understand me?"

I held up the lamp and said, "A little light against the dark, Father. I suggest you get on with it."

Van Horne did not waste further time in argument. He leaned close and said in a calm strong voice, "I want you to make an act of contribution. Say after me: O, my God, who art infinitely good in Thyself . . ."

Jardona, choking in his own blood, followed him, painfully, brokenly, each word a personal Calvary. Step-by-step van Horne moved through the final rites, his voice never faltering and for a while, even the mountain seemed to stop moving and there was silence.

There was a final effusion of blood from Jardona's mouth and his eyes closed. Moreno crossed himself and started to slide out backwards. "Go with God, José," he called softly.

I touched van Horne on the shoulder. He ignored me, leaning over the body, listening, and in the silence I heard slight irregular breathing, Jardona still clinging fast to life. Soil, the merest trickle dribbled out of the shadows, and van Horne, leaning forward to protect the body, started to recite the prayers for the dying.

"Go, Christian soul, from this world, in the Name of God the Father Almighty Who created thee; in the Name of Jesus Christ, the Son of the Living God, Who suffered for thee; in the Name of the Holy Ghost . . ."

With a mighty rush that was like no sound I had

heard before, the mountain shook itself and poured in on us.

Moreno cried out urgently from the tunnel entrance. I grabbed van Horne by the hair and pulled him backwards with all my strength. José Jardona disappeared from sight forever and I scrambled for the way out as fast as any terrified animal seeking a bolt hole.

A flying stone shattered my lamp and I dropped it and crawled into the darkness over rough stones and then Moreno was there, his lamp above his head, a hand outstretched to help me.

I fell to my knees, but got up frantically and turned and when his head and shoulders appeared above me, could not believe it. There was no time for anything but survival now. Moreno and I got an arm apiece and pulled van Horne through, then we ran for our lives as the mountain shook itself above us.

I don't suppose any of those waiting expected to see us emerge from the great cloud of dust that billowed from the entrance, but when we did, there was an incredulous roar and everyone crowded round.

I pushed my way through the press, fell on my hands and knees beside the trough and plunged my head into the cool water. Then I rolled over on my back. I closed my eyes, breathing deeply. When I opened them again, Janos was standing over me.

"By God, sir, but this is really too much," he said. "I was beginning to imagine myself alone in a strange land."

"Van Horne's the man you should talk to," I told him. "He seems to have some sort of death wish, if you ask me. Either that or he's tired of living."

He asked me what had happened and I told him briefly. There was a frown on his face when I had finished, unusual for him. "So, he is taking the part seriously again?"

"When the mood's on him."

"And you?" I frowned in bewilderment. "You stayed also, Mr. Keogh. You could have died, sir, and for what?"

Which was certainly a point. I got up and saw van Horne coming towards us, men easing out of his way, yet staying close, many crossing themselves.

He sluiced water over his head and shoulders and smiled. "We have our moments, Keogh."

But the smile was fleeting and beneath it, there was a new seriousness. He reached for his shirt and Moreno approached, the rest of the men crowding behind. I noticed Jurado lurking on the outskirts of things, obviously waiting to see what was going to happen. I ignored him for the moment, for I was too interested myself.

Moreno said, "What you did in there, Father, for my poor cousin, to ease his going in such terrible circumstances . . . this was a remarkable thing. We are in your debt, all of us. If there is anything we can do . . ."

Van Horne stood looking at them, shirt dangling from one hand, water beading his head and shoulders. I could not see his face, but there was a peculiar quality of stillness to him.

He said clearly, "To mourn the death of one man would be to fly in the face of God's mercy when so many have been saved. I shall hold a service of thanksgiving in the church at two-thirty this afternoon. All who are truly grateful will be there."

There was consternation even on Janos's face. As

for Moreno and his friends, I have seldom seen men more dismayed.

Jurado was already galloping away to bear the glad tidings to his master.

TEN

He gave us no chance to discuss things with him, but announced that he had decided to ride back to Mojada and went off with fifteen or twenty of the miners, including Moreno, who had their own horses or mules. The rest were conveyed in a large waggon pulled by four mules.

Janos and I followed in the buckboard and he was anything but happy about the way things were going. "Did he get knocked on the head down there, by any chance?"

"Several times."

"I thought so. His brain has turned. It can be the only explanation for such madness. De la Plata can't allow a challenge to his power to go unpunished. It would be the beginning of the end for him."

"I suppose that's what van Horne wants. A direct confrontation."

"Which would only have purpose if De la Plata appeared alone and he certainly won't in this instance. If he turns up at the church during the service, he'll have at least a dozen men with him."

"Van Horne must have something up his sleeve," I said. "He certainly isn't doing it just to give De la Plata an excuse to hang him."

"There is another possibility," Janos pointed out. "As I said before, what if he simply can't resist playing the priest?"

An uncomfortable thought and I tried to push it away. "That wouldn't make sense."

"Then explain this morning if you can. He went into the mine with you and Moreno, stayed with that poor devil trapped in the rockfall. Shrived him as well as any priest could from what you tell me and sent him on his way happy. Now why would he do that? Why put his life in jeopardy for no good reason?"

I suddenly realised in a moment of illumination that down there in the dark, I had accepted van Horne for a priest myself, must have done for a while at least, however insane that sounded.

I said lamely, "Oh, I don't know. I went down myself, didn't I?"

"No answer." He smiled. "You see, sir, you are an Irishman and whoever heard of one of that breed ever doing the logical and expected thing in any circumstance?"

Which ended the conversation for the time being for we had reached the hacienda where we were refused admittance to the house by a couple of De la Plata's men standing guard in the courtyard, but allowed to go on our way in the Mercedes.

Janos dozed in the rear seat and I drove glumly down to Mojada trying to make sense out of Oliver van Horne, murderer and thief, who had deliberately walked into that situation at Tacho's to save my neck. Must have done, I saw that now. Who had made me walk proud in the face of imminent death and who could crawl into darkness and extreme danger to hold a dying man's hand and ease his going with prayers which had no validity anyway, although I suppose that was a matter of opinion.

The plain truth was that there was no sense to be found in any of it.

Back at the hotel, I found a sudden and very definite improvement in the service. When we went into the bar, Moreno was already behind the counter. He must have had a bath because there was no sign of the mine about him and he was wearing a clean white shirt and black tie.

He produced a bottle of that special scotch and three glasses and said diffidently, "If you gentlemen will drink with me, I would deem it an honour."

"Very civil of you," Janos said, and we joined him.

Moreno filled the glasses, raised his own in a half-salute. "Señor Keogh, for what you did for my cousin I thank you. In my family's name, I thank you."

I murmured something suitably modest, remembering that family was all important to these people. Moreno said carefully, "Father van Horne, señor—do you think he will do this thing?"

"Tomás de la Plata warned him against holding any kind of service," I said. "That's all I know."

"Hardly our affair," Janos put in.

"You think there will be trouble?" I asked Moreno.

"Don Tomás will kill him if he holds that service, señor, nothing is more certain. He will kill anyone who takes part. I tried to tell Father van Horne this when we rode in from the mine together, but he refused to discuss the matter."

"With you perhaps, but not with us." Janos emptied his glass and glanced at me. "Dammit, Mr. Keogh, but we can't let the fellow hang himself for no sensible reason known to man, now can we?"

"I suppose not," I said, playing his game.

"Don't worry, Moreno," he said cheerfully. "We'll talk some sense into him."

Moreno was pathetically grateful and escorted us outside, opening the rear door of the Mercedes and handing Janos in. I suppose that as mayor of Mojada he simply didn't want any unnecessary trouble. On the other hand, van Horne had made his mark, there was no doubt about that.

I drove up through the village towards the church. There was no sign of van Horne, but as I braked to a halt, hooves clattered over the stony ground and I turned to see Victoria pulling in her mount, Nachita behind her. She ran forward, concern on her face, reached out to touch me in a dozen different places as if to assure herself no bones were broken.

I said to Nachita, "You heard about what happened at the mine?"

"I was in to buy supplies at the store, señor, they talk of little else."

I took her hands in mine. "I have business now with the priest. I'll come down to the camp later." She frowned as if uncertain or distrusting me, so I kissed her on the mouth in spite of the company. "Now go or I'll tie you across your horse."

She smiled delightfully, vaulted into the saddle, wheeled her horse in a tight circle and galloped away so fast that she caught Nachita off-balance. He was actually a couple of yards in the rear as he went after her.

"At least she does what you tell her," Janos observed.

"Only sometimes."

I helped him out and when we turned to the church,

van Horne was standing in the porch dressed in a cassock and clerical collar and wearing a black birreta, something else which must have come from the trunk.

"I wondered how long it would be."

He moved to the Mercedes, got in the back and raised the seat. There was a large piece of felt underneath which he removed, revealing bare metal. It proved to be a false bottom for he got his fingers into some special place and lifted, disclosing a tin box painted khaki with United State Army Ordnance painted on the cover in black.

He picked it up in both hands. "You'd better come inside, and don't forget the cigar," he added to Janos.

The Hungarian sighed and tossed the cigar away reluctantly. "Don't you think you are taking this all a little too far?"

Van Horne ignored the remark and led the way in. The worst of the charcoal obscenities had been scraped from the walls although he hadn't got round to giving them a coat of whitewash yet. The smell of dirt and decay I had noticed only yesterday was almost gone. Down at the altar, the crucifix glinted, a candle on either side and it was peaceful. It was a church again.

Van Horne put the box down on a bench and opened it. Janos said, "Keogh and I would like to know what the game is. You are not on your own in this and time you realised that."

Van Horne looked enquiringly at me. I said, "No one will come. They don't dare."

"Tomás de la Plata will come," he said. "And that is all that matters. He'll come to gloat at my failure and very possibly to kill me."

"But not on his own, man," Janos insisted urgently. "Why should he?"

Van Horne said, "Two days, that's all he gave us. After this morning's fiasco at the mine, why should he indulge us further. The showdown must be now and on our terms."

"He never goes anywhere without at least a dozen men at his back," I pointed out.

Van Horne walked to the other end of the church and mounted into the pulpit. He stood facing us, hands on either side of a small wooden lectern on which I noticed he had placed a Bible.

"When he and his friends walk in, this is where they will find me and they'll never know what hit them."

His hands dipped out of sight, re-appeared clutching the machine gun. God save us all, but he looked like the Angel of Death himself up there and it would work—I could see that. See Tomás de la Plata and his men walk into the empty church, could hear the jingle of the spurs, the jeers. I had seen van Horne in action remember. Knew only too well how devastating a weapon a Thompson gun became in his hands. Tomás de la Plata and those with him would be dead before they knew it.

There was one snag that I could see and Janos voiced it. "What if he leaves some of his men outside, sir, what then?"

"That's where you and Keogh come in. You'll be on the first floor of the bell tower, twenty feet up, with a clear field of fire."

"With what?" I demanded.

"Look in the box."

I did and found a dozen Mills bombs, a sawn-off, double-barrelled shotgun, a Winchester repeater, at least a thousand rounds of ammunition and a Thompson gun that was twin to his own.

I drove Janos back to the hotel, dropped him there and left the village on foot for I wanted time to think.

Van Horne's plan was well enough, a dangerous, bloody ambush that had every chance of working, just as he had indicated. With the two machine guns and a grenade or two lobbed down from the tower, it was more than likely that we could kill or cripple every last one of them within seconds.

In the final analysis it all depended on Tomás de la Plata behaving as expected, which was hardly the most cheerful of thoughts. In the past, I had waited in ambush too many times for those who did not come or came another way and the change from hunter to quarry was easily made.

The pack horses and mules had gone, that was the first thing I noted as I approached the Yaqui encampment, but the tent was still there beside the fire, four horses grazing nearby.

There was a leather-bound book on a blanket by the fire. I picked it up and opened it. It was a copy of *Don Quixote* in Spanish. There was no greater sound than a breeze might make through grass and when I glanced up, Nachita was watching.

"A fine book, señor."

"Yours?" I said.

"As a youth I spent some time with the Fathers at Nacozari. For a while they talked of making me a priest, but my own voices spoke to me of different things and I returned to my people. A man has but one life to live."

I dropped the book back on the blanket. "Where are the others?"

"Gone, señor, across the mountains with the pack animals."

"But you stay?"

He smiled, or at least his face moved in what for him was the nearest equivalent to such a thing. "She is waiting by the pool on the other side of the cottonwoods, señor."

He dropped to the ground with a kind of easy grace, picked up *Don Quixote* and opened it, so I left him to the delights of great literature and went in search of different pleasures.

It was a pretty place. A waterfall dropping twenty or thirty feet into a small pool surrounded by great tilted slabs of stone. She sat on an old horse blanket, knees drawn up to her chin and stared into space, caught in some private place of her own, yet she knew it was me and was on her feet at the first footfall.

She stood looking at me warily as if expecting some visible sign of something, although of what, I had no idea. I said quietly, "It is good to see you. Good to be alone with you."

She smiled gravely and yet there was a slight frown on her face, a wariness, as if faced with something she did not fully understand. Above us clouds spilled out from the mountains, obscuring the sun for a little while and it was quiet there by the water at the edge of the trees, more quiet than I had thought it possible to be and cold. I found myself shaking violently and something even colder thrust like a sword into the deepest part of me.

It was a thing I had known on more than one occasion, the Celt in me again, and always before bad things happened. And she, God bless her, knew, understood in some strange way of her own, reached out and pulled my hands hard against her breasts.

"I know," I said. "I'm afraid. It happens to the best of us. Even to little Emmet Keogh, Emmet of the good left hand."

She was frowning now and I pulled her down on the blanket and kissed her lips. "Edmundo—Edmundo Keogh. Would you like to hear about him?"

She nodded, half-smiling, still wary. "I've a grandfather back home who would bless the day he met you," I told her. "He always did say God's greatest gift to Man was a beautiful woman who could keep a still tongue in her head."

She liked that, her smile said as much. Probably even liked the sound of him and it was as good a place to start as any. So I began to talk, a monologue to end all monologues, the personal testament of little Emmet Keogh. A story that took in most things and I shirked none of it. They all received an honourable mention. Big Mick Collins, the men I had killed for good reason or bad, my own brother included. By the time I had finished she knew all there was to know about our bargain with Bonilla, as much about van Horne and Janos as I knew myself.

All this I told her because out of some strange foreknowledge, I knew van Horne's plan was not going to work. Knew it for no logical reason possible to man, but could not prove it.

I lay with my head in her lap quietly, at peace at last, all talk ended and gazed into a sky of limitless blue and her fingers gently stroked my forehead, easing me into sleep. Her deliberate intention, I am certain, and she would have left me so, but I came awake with a start at the first note of the church bell, the bell which van Horne had said he would ring half-an-hour before the service.

She did not try to stop me and I did not kiss her in parting, the thing was too deep for that now. I simply looked at her for a long and final moment, then turned and walked away through the trees towards whatever waited for me in the heat of the afternoon.

Janos was on the verandah at the front of the hotel and came to me cheerfully, suggesting a walk, the remark obviously being intended for Moreno who sat in a cane chair looking thoroughly worried.

"He doesn't seem too happy," I commented.

Janos smiled. "His wife is, I understand, in labour, though whether at this precise moment in time he is worrying more about her than van Horne is a matter of doubt." He blew out a cloud of cigar smoke with a sigh of content. "Really a most excellent afternoon. Good to be alive."

I could never decide to what extent he said things for effect and yet on the whole, I am inclined to feel that his nonchalance was not studied, but real. The plain truth is that he was one of those odd people who really did live in the here and now and for whom the future and its prospects held few terrors for it simply did not exist.

We strolled casually through the village by the east wall, coming in the end, to the rear of the church where we were admitted by van Horne at the back door which led directly into the vestry.

He wore a white linen alb over his cassock and now, he put on a green stole, crossing it under his girdle to represent Christ's Passion and Death, as I remembered. The green chasuble came next and he was ready.

"I must say you look the part, sir," Janos told him.

"I damn well better do," van Horne replied grimly. "About fifteen minutes to go, so the sooner you two get up that tower, the better."

He took us out through the church and opened a small wooden door at the rear of the pulpit, which I had never noticed before, disclosing a stone spiral staircase.

"You'll find everything you need up there," he said. "Just remember one thing. You fire when I do. No private parties, no matter how it looks to you from up there. We want this thing to turn out just one way."

The door slammed and I went up through the half-darkness behind Janos who was making such heavy weather of the steep and narrow stairs that I had to put both hands to his back and push.

We made it and found ourselves in a room perhaps ten feet square with long narrow windows on three sides reaching almost to the floor. Everything was ready for us as van Horne had promised, laid out neatly on a blanket. The shotgun with ammunition, the Winchester, several Mills bombs and the Thompson gun, half-a-dozen drum magazines in a neat pile beside it.

Janos collapsed on a wooden bench struggling for breath, sweat pouring from him. He took a flask from one of his pockets, unscrewed the top and had a long swallow as I examined our situation.

There was one snag. The position of the windows in the wall on the side which counted made it impossible to see down into the village itself unless one leaned out, although it gave a clear view of the immediate area around the porch twenty feet below and a little to one side.

I showed Janos, who seemed himself again, how

things stood and he nodded soberly. "That means we won't be able to see him coming so we had better be ready."

I moved a bench, positioning it against the wall by the window so that Janos could sit in comfort, out of sight and yet with a clear view of the area around the porch. I gave him the Thompson gun and he nursed it on his knees, a cigar between his teeth. My intention was to support him with two or three judiciously placed Mills bombs and, if necessary, the Enfield or the Winchester. The shot-gun, because of the shortness of its barrels, didn't seem much of a proposition.

There was a single narrow slit, some nine inches wide, in the wall with no windows. When I peered through I found myself looking down into the pulpit, the church beyond. There was no sign of van Horne and then the vestry door opened and he came out holding the Thompson gun. He turned towards the pulpit, which meant that he now faced the altar and, as I watched, he genuflected smoothly, automatically crossing himself, then mounted into the pulpit, his face impassive.

"And what, my dear sir, would you make of that?" Janos breathed in my ear.

Van Horne placed the Thompson carefully on a small shelf where it would come to hand, sat down on a stool and opened the Bible. I straightened and shook my head. "God knows," I said and meant it. "I no longer try to understand him. I just accept."

It was very quiet and far too hot. Janos wiped sweat from his face and sighed. "I'm not built for this kind of thing any more."

"But you were once." It was a statement, not a question. As much for the sake of conversation as anything else.

"When I first came to Mexico I served as cavalry adviser to a federal force that was trying to exterminate the Yaqui in the mountains north of here and finding it hard work, in spite of the fact that the going rate for a Yaqui warrior's ears was one hundred pesos."

"They must have wanted rid of them pretty badly."

"The government wanted their land, it was as simple as that, which explains why the survivors now live in areas like the Wind River country where no one else could. This all took place in the bad old days under Diaz."

"And afterwards?"

"In the early days of the Revolution I served with Francisco Madero at the taking of Ciudad Juárez. There were many like myself. What he called his foreign legion. Men like the great Garibaldi's nephew, Giuseppe. A fine soldier."

"You must have had some interesting experiences."

"Indeed, but then they murdered Madero, or that at least is my own interpretation of what happened. Too good to live, poor man. If he'd been harder on the rogues that needed it. Dark days, sir. One never quite knew who to follow next."

Hooves rattled on the cobbles of the street out of sight to the right of us, laughter drifted up on the warm air, the jingle of harness. When they rode into view, I saw that we had all miscalculated woefully for there were at least two dozen of them, each man an arsenal in himself.

Tomás de la Plata was in the centre, as dark and sombre a figure as usual and greatest shock of all, his sister rode at his right hand.

ELEVEN

He had brought her to witness van Horne's humiliation and for no other reason that I could see. She looked white and strained and came off her horse with considerable unwillingness when he reached up for her. He took her by the arm and went into the porch, seven or eight of his men following.

"Now what happens?" Janos whispered.

I moved to the slit in the wall and peered into the church. Van Horne was still seated only now the Thompson gun was ready across his knees. There was the rattle of spurs, a burst of laughter and De la Plata walked in, his arm around Chela's shoulders.

"Business is not so good today, Father?" he called.

Van Horne put the Thompson gun back on the shelf very carefully and stood up. "It would appear so. Does that give you satisfaction?"

"To discover that pigs behave predictably? Not particularly." De la Plata looked down at his sister whom he still held tightly. "Does it give you any satisfaction, my love?"

There was something unpleasant here, something under the surface that should not be. She tried to pull free of him, but he held her tight. "You must forgive her, Father. Strange under the circumstances, but she was not anxious to come here. She only did so under my persuasion."

Behind him, his men ranged in a line, rifles cradled carelessly, a perfect target, yet van Horne would not try now, not with the woman there and if I disobeyed his orders and tried to pick off De la Plata himself, the return fire of his men must be met and Chela in the middle of it.

I could not see van Horne's face, but his voice was quite calm when he said, "What do you want with me, señor? My death?"

"Not necessary." Tomás de la Plata shook his head. "You will go, priest. Tomorrow you will leave the way you came with those who brought you. I would hang you with pleasure, but unfortunately I gave my sister my word and if she keeps hers, I will keep mine."

He turned and swept out, his arm still tight around her shoulders and his men trooped after him, the last one spitting on the floor. Van Horne went down the steps of the pulpit and hurried after him.

I got to the window just as Tomás de la Plata swung into the saddle beside his sister. As his men moved in around them, the whole group started to turn away.

Van Horne appeared from the porch and shouted, "Señor de la Plata. A word with you."

Don Tomás reined in his horse and the others followed suit. "What do you want?"

Van Horne spoke clearly so that all might hear. "I have in my possession the image of the Blessed St. Martin de Porres taken from this church during the Revolution. In these circumstances, before replacing such a relic in its rightful place, it is usual to carry it in procession through the town."

Only the nervous stamping of a horse broke the

stillness as all waited for what was to follow.

"I intend to make that procession at nine-thirty to-morrow morning starting from the church."

Chela gave a short, anguished cry, stilled by her brother in an instant. "There is not a soul in this village who would take that walk with you."

"Then I walk alone."

Tomás de la Plata drew the pistol from under his jacket very fast and I snatched the Thompson from Janos in the same instant, ready to fire if needs be, Chela or no Chela, although even van Horne was too close for comfort now.

Chela cried out, a hand on her brother's arm and I think for a moment, things hung in the balance. He pushed the gun back into its shoulder holster.

"I keep my words, priest," he said. "You have until tomorrow at noon to go and live. As for this walk of yours. Try to take that and I kill you myself."

"Alone or with your men at your back?"

Tomás de la Plata's eyes glittered. His face was pale as white fire, but he said not another word, gave the signal and the whole group moved away.

I took a chance, leaning out of the window to watch them go, caught a glimpse of people standing in a ragged line fifteen or twenty yards away and drew back quickly.

"It seems he had an audience."

"By God, sir, I can believe anything," Janos replied.

I went down the spiral staircase, Janos following more slowly, and hurried along to the main entrance, pausing in the porch to peer cautiously through the side window which was minus its glass.

The crowd was fading away and beyond them, De la Plata and his men were already passing through the gate. Van Horne walked in through the porch rapidly, brushing past me as if I wasn't there. He pulled his chasuble over his head and threw it down on the nearest bench, then started to take off his alb.

"Quite a performance," I said, as Janos approached.

Van Horne turned on me, anger and frustration bursting out of him. "And what would you have had me do, Keogh? Kill the woman?"

"Never mind that," I said, evading an answer. "What about this other nonsense? This procession with that damned image. De la Plata was right. There isn't a man, woman or child in this village who dares to take that walk with you."

"Then I'll take it alone."

"And hope you'll shame de la Plata into barring your way on his own? He doesn't play those sort of games."

He did not reply and yet a muscle worked in his cheek, the great hands clenching and unclenching and there was something between us, something which could not be put into words. I knew and I think he did also.

I moved close and said in a low urgent voice, "Why, van Horne? Why?"

"Damn you, Keogh, I don't even know the answer to that one myself." He flung the alb to one side, turned and walked down to the vestry.

There was really nothing to say after that. Janos and I left him and went down to the hotel. There was no sign of Moreno in the bar so I went behind and served us both with a whisky.

"Now what?" Janos demanded.

"Don't ask me, ask him."

He sighed morosely. "You know something, my

friend? It doesn't look good. It doesn't look good at all."

He reached for the bottle and helped himself to another drink and I left him there, went round to the rear courtyard where I had parked the Mercedes and drove back up the hill towards the church.

I had remembered the arms left in the bell tower. In his present mood van Horne would probably forget them and they were better in a safe place. I suppose the real truth was that I wanted to have another crack at him. I was wasting my time for as I reached the top of the hill, I passed him on his way down with Moreno.

I brought the arms down from the tower anyway, repacked them in the box, took it out to the Mercedes and put it back in its hiding place under the seat.

I returned to the church, sat on a bench and looked down towards the altar. All right, so I could manage without God these days, but it was peaceful in there in the half-light with the candles winking at the altar.

Victoria Balbuena appeared in the doorway. She paused, looking at me searchingly, automatically covering her head with a square of cotton and tying it under her chin.

I took her hands, smiling as I pulled her down beside me. "See, I survive all things."

We could take it no further. There was a shout outside, running feet and van Horne appeared in the doorway. The Enfield was already in my hand.

He said, "You won't need that. It's Moreno's wife. She's in a bad way. The baby won't come and the old woman who's midwife round here doesn't seem to know what to do."

I sat there, staring at him. He got me by the front

of the jacket and had me on my feet in an instant.
"Good God, boy, did you spend four years training to
be a doctor or didn't you?"

When I drove up to the hotel, there was a crowd of
thirty or forty people outside for bad news travels fast.
I told Victoria to come with me and we followed van
Horne, who pushed his way through ruthlessly.

The scene in the bedroom was unbelievable. At
least a dozen people, all close relatives, the women already mourning their loudest, Moreno with tears in
his eyes and unable to control any of it.

The wretched woman on the bed was covered with
a sheet and obviously terrified out of her life, crying
hysterically. The old crone who leaned over her, presumably the midwife, was without a doubt the dirt-
iest-looking creature I'd seen in many a long day.

"Get them out," I told van Horne. "All of them.
The midwife can stay as long as she washes her hands.
Tell them I want hot water from the kitchen instantly
and soap."

They went, protesting, although Moreno already
counted her dead and I heard him say so brokenly as
he went backwards through the door.

"Then pray for her," van Horne said calmly.
"Pray that the Blessed St. Martin de Porres might
intercede for her."

He closed the door, then went swiftly to the windows which stood open to the terrace, for the crowd
was beginning to get noisy. I couldn't hear what he
said to them, presumably something similar, but it
certainly shut them up and he came in and closed the
windows.

There was a tap at the door, Victoria opened it
and returned with a pan of water and a block of

cheap, carbolic soap. I started to wash my hands and told the old woman to do the same. Her only reply was to throw up her hands and run out of the room.

I pulled the sheet back over the woman's belly, pushed up her knees and made my examination, discovering immediately the reason for the old mid-wife's dismay.

"Can you still remember how?" van Horne asked.

We spoke in English for the mother's sake. I said, "A baby's normally delivered head-first. This is what's known as a breech. That means it's presenting its backside which is one hell of a complication."

"But can you handle it?" he said urgently.

"Let's say I've studied the theory."

The woman started to yell, I moved to her side and tried to calm her. It didn't do much good and van Horne went round to the other side and took her hand. "There is nothing to worry about, I promise you," he said. "Soon it will be all over and you will have your son."

There was that quality in his voice again. Compassion, love, call it what you will and complete authority. The woman's crying subsided into little broken sobs, but she would not let go of his hand, gazing up at him with complete trust.

I took Victoria into the corner, explained to her very rapidly in a low voice what I was going to try to do and her part in it and then I got to work.

I needed the woman as close to the edge of the bed as possible to facilitate the work, so to speak. We moved her between us which started her off again until van Horne quietened her.

In my time under training, I had delivered half-a-dozen children, all perfectly straightforward cases. I had only once seen the type of delivery I was going to attempt now, and that in hospital, but had naturally studied the theory of the thing as I had informed van Horne. I took the deepest of breaths and tried to remember, stage-by-stage as I might if confronted by the examiners.

The first problem was to deliver the legs and success in that area depends upon them being flexed. I probed gently and found, as might have been expected, that the legs were extended. Which meant more patient probing until I could get a finger up against the back of one of the child's knees and prod. The leg flexed instantly and so did the other when I repeated the performance.

Señora Moreno gave a startled cry, her body shook convulsively. I told her to start pushing. A moment later, the legs delivered themselves.

Victoria had torn a linen sheet into several pieces and was standing by. I held out my hands and she wiped them clean and dried them quickly. I turned to begin the next stage.

I grasped the legs, fingers beneath the thighs and thumbs on the sacrum and pulled down until the shoulders were in sight. Now the arms were extended, but I remembered how to handle that one too. I twisted the child gently to the left. The shoulder flexed, I hooked a finger into the left elbow and delivered the arm. Then I rotated in the opposite direction and carried out the same manoeuvre for the other arm.

I paused to take breath and van Horne said in English, "How is it going?"

"Fine so far, but I'm just coming into the most dangerous stage. Delivery of the head. Tricky even with instruments. There is a very real chance of brain damage unless it's done just right."

The secret was to bring out the head slowly and steadily and I remembered the procedure exactly. I put my right arm beneath the child and got my forefinger into its mouth which meant I was now supporting it on my forearm.

Next, I placed the forefinger of my left hand on the head to flex it and the index and ring fingers on the right and left shoulders respectively and started to exert traction. Slowly, very slowly, it began to move and yet the strength I had to exert was so considerable that sweat stood on my forehead in great drops.

And then it was clear and safe in my hands although it became obvious at once that it was not breathing. The whole body was a rather unpleasant deep purple as if everything was locked up and waiting to move.

I tried slapping it with no immediate result, so took a small piece of cotton Victoria passed me, cleared the mouth and nostrils of mucus and liquor. The heartbeat was strong, so there was nothing wrong there.

Very gently, I blew into the tiny mouth. Quite suddenly the child took a convulsive breath, then, most beautiful sound in all the world, it started to cry.

For some reason Victoria was crying too, although she took the child from me competently enough and held him while I saw to the placenta and checked the woman's own state, now that it was all over.

"A boy," I announced. "If anyone is interested."

Van Horne took the child, which Victoria had wrapped carefully in a linen sheet, and moved to the bedside. I didn't hear what he said to Señora Moreno, but I know she started to cry again and said brokenly, "Just as you promised, Father. Just as you promised."

He put the baby down beside her, opened the windows and went out on the terrace. All very dramatic and there was a satisfying outcry from the crowd in the street.

I seemed rather unnecessary, which was fair enough, because that is exactly what I was. I got up, went to the door and opened it just as Moreno appeared with the womenfolk behind him. They pressed past me into the room, making the kind of sounds one would have expected and I left them to it and went along the corridor to my own room.

God, but I was tired, more than I had been in years and yet strangely happy. For once I had given life instead of taking it, I suppose, although I was no longer able to think straight.

I lay on the bed, staring up at the ceiling and the door opened and Victoria came in. She sat beside me and gently smoothed my brow, untying the knots one-by-one and very gradually, I drifted into sleep.

TWELVE

I awakened to darkness, the pulsating beat of music. Guitars and maracas from the sound of it and someone was singing. I was alone, for there was no sign of Victoria, even when I swung my feet to the floor, found a match and lit the lamp. My boots were at the end of the bed. I pulled them on, went to the washstand in the corner, leaned over the bowl and emptied the earthenware jug of water over my head.

Which made me feel a lot better. I found a towel, opened a window and went out on the terrace and stood there, breathing in the cool night air and drying myself at the same time. The light from the hotel windows spilled out across the street and showed me Victoria and Nachita sitting on the edge of the boardwalk opposite.

"Victoria," I called softly and she looked up. "Why did you leave me? Come on up."

Her face was a pale blur indicating nothing. Nachita answered for her. "It is not permitted, señor."

"What in the hell are you talking about?" I demanded. "Wait for me there. I'll be right down."

I found a clean shirt, pulled it over my head and went downstairs. I didn't bother going into the bar, but went straight out through the front door and plunged across the street without looking so that a couple of horsemen had to rein-in to avoid hitting me.

Victoria and Nachita rose to meet me and I took her by the arms. "What's all this about?"

Nachita said, "She was asked to leave the hotel, señor."

"That's nonsense," I told him.

"In Mojada it is not so bad." He shrugged. "I know places where an Indian, especially a Yaqui, would not be allowed in town limits."

And inside, the bastards were celebrating. The two horsemen had dismounted and were staring across at us. I recognised Jurado, but the other was a stranger to me. Jurado made some comment or other and laughed and then turned and went inside, closing the door behind him.

It was very quiet, the music muted and far away and I was no longer tired, only angry in a sad sort of way and sorry for humanity, if you understand me.

I raised her hands to my lips and said, "Wait for me here. I'll get a jacket and walk back to the camp with you."

The door to the bar was open as I went through the hall and as I passed, I heard van Horne bellow, "Keogh, in here."

I paused in the doorway. I should think just about every man in the village was in there and most of them with drink taken. Four musicians were banging away briskly in the corner.

Van Horne and Janos were at a table, jammed up tight against the bar and the Hungarian raised his glass. "To the hero of the hour. Join us, sir, I insist."

I stood at the bar beside them, Jurado and his friend behind me, which was important in view of what happened. Moreno was dispensing free drinks, himself half-drunk. Van Horne glanced up at me.

"You don't look pleased, Keogh, what's wrong?"

"I understand they threw Victoria out when I was asleep."

He shrugged. "A custom of the country. She's chosen her side, Keogh, and the plain fact is that the average Mexican can't stand Indians."

"Especially Yaqui," Janos put in. "Incredibly cruel people, Keogh. When I served with that federal punitive expedition we had a colonel called Cubero who'd bought himself a harem of five Yaqui women. Women, I say. As I remember, the eldest was only fifteen. A hundred pesos each."

"And you call the Yaqui cruel?" I said.

"They ambushed him with a patrol in the mountains one day." Janos was as drunk as I had seen him and spoke rather slowly as a consequence. "God knows what they'd done to him before they finished him off, but when we found him, he had an eyeball in the palm of each hand and his private parts had been stuffed between his teeth."

"What do you expect me to do, vomit?" I demanded. "I'd say he got what he deserved at a hundred pesos each for little girls."

Moreno leaned across the bar, grinning foolishly. "Heh, Señor Keogh, we have decided to name the boy for Father van Horne. A good idea, you agree?"

"I think it's bloody marvellous." I turned to van Horne. "Another van Horne miracle, is that how it turned out?"

His smile died, something close to pain in his eyes and Moreno touched my arm. "You will drink with me, señor?"

"No thanks," I said. "I've made other arrangements."

He seemed genuinely bewildered. "But I don't understand, señor."

I had not buttoned my shirt and the silver amulet Victoria had given me swung free. Jurado reached across and took it in his fingers. "It is very simple, Moreno. Señor Keogh prefers other company to ours. Darker meat." He laughed coarsely. "Is it true what they say about Yaqui women?" He followed this with probably the most obscene suggestion I had heard in my life.

I think I knew then that he was there to make trouble. Not particularly with me, but I had come easily to hand, so to speak. Van Horne started to get up and I shoved him back into his chair.

"I'd be very happy to drink with you," I said to Moreno. "In a moment."

As I turned and walked out, Jurado laughed. "Ah, the little one runs to avoid messing his pants." One or two of the drunks laughed dutifully.

Victoria and Nachita crossed the street to meet me. I said, "I've been invited to have a drink before I go."

She knew what was in my mind, I saw it in her eyes and so did Nachita. He said, "There is nothing to be gained from this, señor, they would spit on us."

A strange thing happened then. I went very cold, very calm, fire in my belly and when I spoke, the voice came from somewhere outside me and the sound of it would have frightened Finn Cuchulain himself.

"You will listen to me now," I said. "I am Emmet Keogh of Stradballa and afraid of no man on this earth. We will go now and God will go with us. I will see justice done and if I must break a head or two in the process, then well enough."

The blackness was in me then as it had been in my

father, so they tell me. The violence there had been no escaping, that had sent my mother to an early grave. I turned without another word and they followed and when I reached the door, I kicked it open and went in like a strong wind. The silence had to be heard to be believed when they saw what stood behind me.

I walked to the bar, put my hands on the edge and confronted poor foolish Moreno, mouth agape. "I'll have that drink now."

I half-turned, leaning against the bar, back to van Horne and Janos, facing Jurado and his friend. Victoria stood a yard or two away and smiled when I looked at her. I raised my fingers to my lips and kissed them. There was a gasp from someone in the crowd. I saw Nachita's fingers ready in the lever of his old Winchester.

Moreno put a bottle on the bar, his good whisky, and one glass. I said, "You are forgetting my friends."

There was a look of agony on his face. Poor devil, he didn't know what to do next. Jurado solved the situation for him. His great hand wrapped itself round the neck of the bottle. "No," he said.

That close, the smell of him, his gross body, was quite overpowering. I said, "Did anyone ever tell you that you stink, my friend?"

There was genuine amazement in his eyes, shock that someone dare insult him so before everyone there. Especially a man so much smaller than himself.

He released the bottle in a kind of reflex gesture and I picked it up and smashed it across the side of his head. As he cried out, staggering back, I wrenched the pistol from his holster and tossed it to van Horne.

Jurado started to turn, blood on his face and I grabbed the nearest chair and smashed it across the great head and shoulders. Once, twice and then again, breaking it apart.

He fell on his knees and stayed there for a while, then got up and stood looking at me, one hand wiping blood away mechanically.

"All right then, you bastard," I said, dropping into a fighting crouch. "Let's be having you."

My grandfather, they tell me, might have been a contender for the heavyweight crown had he so chosen and in his youth, had gone the distance with the great Bob Fitzsimmons himself.

From my earliest years at school, my small size earned me more kicks than halfpence. For some time this went undetected for I have always been considered close by nature, and then an ambush by a couple of tinker's boys one fine evening sent me home with a face like raw meat.

Mickeen Bawn Keogh examined that face, his grey eyes cold and rather frightening in spite of the smile on his face. "Two of them, did you say, *avic?*" He nodded. "Then it is time I took you in hand and long overdue."

Whereupon he took off his jacket, led me out into the yard and gave me my first lesson in the noble art and no holds barred.

So I was only five and a half feet and weighed barely ten stone, but I could punch every pound of it as Raul Jurado found to his cost that night.

He came in with a roar, I feinted with my left and smashed my right fist into his mouth, splitting the lips so that blood spurted. I followed it with a left below the breast that sounded like the crack of a whip when bone met bone.

Footwork, timing and hitting, that was the secret and in that first couple of minutes I gave him neither quarter nor peace, circling around, evading his ponderous blows with ease, feinting and jabbing, in and away again.

The crowd scattered, most of them scrambling for the door and there was a press of faces at the windows outside. Janos still sat at the table, hands folded on the knob of his stick, face shining with sweat, but van Horne was standing now, Jurado's pistol in his right hand.

I suppose I got careless, forgetting the rawhide quirt dangling from Jurado's wrist. I danced in to belt him again and he slashed out blindly, the rawhide curling around my face, drawing an involuntary cry of agony from me.

Worst of all, when he pulled, I had no choice but to lurch towards him and he delivered a stunning blow to my forehead that sent me back towards the bar. His friend stuck out a foot putting me flat on my back.

I rolled away as Jurado came in fast, boot raised to crush my face. I grabbed for that foot, twisted and he fell heavily across me. We rolled here and there between the tables trying to have each other's eyes out and when we stopped, I was on top.

He got his knee into me before I could do any damage and threw me backwards with a powerful kick. As I scrambled up, he rose to meet me, his face a mask of blood and I was not afraid. As I circled, I saw Victoria by the door, teeth bared like any she-cat, Nachita holding her arm.

Jurado was going to kill me now, it was in his face. His hands came up, hooked into claws and he charged like a bull. I threw a chair into his path that put him on his knees and kicked him in the side of the head.

He stayed there on his hands and knees for the second time that night and his friend at the bar, thinking, I suppose, that I would finish him off, pulled out his pistol. He was fast, but not fast enough. Two foot of steel flashed from the Hungarian's stick, blurred in motion. Jurado's friend dropped his pistol with a cry, blood spurting as he grabbed his wrist.

Even then, Jurado surprised me by the sheer bull-strength of him. He came in low, his shoulder sending me back against the wall. His foot slipped or I think he might have had me. As I straightened, he lurched forward again. I ducked under his arm, twisted a shoulder inwards and sent him over my hip through the window in a savage cross-buttock.

The crowd scattered in a snowstorm of flying glass and I scrambled over the sill and arrived on the terrace in time to put my boot in his face as he tried to get up, sending him back into the street.

He lay there on his back and I suddenly found it necessary to hang on to one of the verandah posts. I turned, leaning against it, and found Victoria on the edge of the crowd four or five yards away.

Her face seemed very pale, the eyes enormous. I smiled, or thought I did, though my face must have looked a sight and then, dear God above us, a miracle happened.

Her eyes filled with horror, her face shattered like a mirror breaking, the mouth opened wide in what should have been a soundless scream. Instead, she cried my name.

"Emm-et!" Broken in the centre, yet quite unmistakable.

I turned and swung to one side as Jurado lunged in,

a knife in one hand. In the same moment, Nachita appeared from the darkness behind him and flung his own knife underhand so that it thudded into the boardwalk at my feet.

By God, but the power was in me then. Such release as I had never known to hear my name spoken by the one person who mattered most. She told me much later, that when I went down into the street to meet him, knife in hand, the look on my face was terrible to see.

Jurado must have agreed for he threw his own knife away from him and staggered into the darkness.

I swung round, challenging that sea of faces, yellow in the lamplight, fear on most of them and then van Horne stepped down and put a hand to my chest as if to stop me falling. His voice seemed to come from under the earth itself, remote, far away, but in any case, there was only one person I wished to see at that moment.

For some reason she was crying. Now why would that be? And then I remembered. I said gently, "My name? What's my name?"

But there was nothing to fear for the spell was broken. "Emm-et," she said. "Emm-et."

"We will go now," I said. "Before I fall down and disgrace us all in the face of the world."

She took one arm, Nachita the other and we left them there and went to our own place.

They got me to the camp and into the tent and I lay there in the cool darkness and let the night wash over me. After a while, Victoria came back with a bowl of water and a cloth. She started to gently wipe my face.

I was tired, my head adrift from my shoulders, but I was still conscious enough to need reassuring and took her by the wrists. "Speak to me—anything. Just let me hear your voice."

There was a hesitation I could almost feel and then slowly, hesitantly, each word separate, the voice rather remote and more than a little hoarse, she said, "What do you want me to say?"

"Not another word," I answered and started to laugh weakly and then the darkness really did close in on me.

I awakened to firelight flickering on the canvas walls of the tent and to voices. It took me a moment or so, not only to think back to reality, but to realise that one of them was van Horne.

I crawled out through the entrance, so stiff and sore that it was past belief and found the three of them sitting by the fire drinking coffee. Nachita saw me first and van Horne and Victoria turned in the same moment.

She was beside me in a flash, helping me stand. "You should be resting."

There was still that faintly unreal flavour to her speech. Van Horne said, "How do you feel?"

"Like a very old hound-dog."

"That was quite a performance. You can use yourself." My Enfield in its holster was lying beside him and he picked it up. "I noticed you'd left this in your room. Thought you might be needing it." There was more to it than that, of course. Had to be.

"Where's Janos?"

"Oh, he decided to have an early night."

My head still felt swollen and somehow disembodied and I was having difficulty in thinking straight and that would not do at all.

"I need to clear my head," I said. "And there's only one way I'm going to do that in a hurry. I won't be long."

The moon was full, the cottonwoods a maze of light and shadow and beyond, the waterfall was silver in the moonlight as it cascaded over rocks.

I stripped and stood there for a moment, the night wind cold on my flesh, feeling for the bruises gingerly and any sign of real damage. My ribs and the rest of me seemed intact enough and I moved out across a patch of shingle and waded into the water.

It was cold enough to freeze the marrow in the bones or so it seemed. I swallowed a howl and swam to the other side and back again. The effects were remarkably bracing and I stood under the waterfall for a moment or so, for the pool was nowhere more than four feet deep as far as I could judge.

Ten seconds of that icy deluge was all I could stand and when I waded out to the shingle strand, van Horne was standing watching me, the Enfield in his hand.

"You forgot this again." He shook his head. "That's what women do to a man, Keogh. The beginning of the end."

"True enough," I said, catching the blanket he tossed me. "But what an end."

He smiled. "So your brains are unscrambled again? That's a blessing. Do you try to commit suicide often?"

I shrugged as I rubbed myself down. "You know how it is."

He paused in the act of lighting one of his cigarillos, the match flaring in his hand. "I'm not sure that I do."

"I don't like to be leaned on," I said. "To be

shoved against the wall. Brings out the worst in me and men like Jurado do, certainly. Probably something to do with my size."

"I had noticed," he replied, a touch of irony in his voice.

I pulled on my shirt and found a crumpled packet of Artistas in my trouser pocket. "What did you want to see me about?"

He seemed surprised. "Why, tomorrow, of course. What else?"

"You still intend to go through with it, this walk nonsense?"

"I'll be outside the church at nine-thirty just like I said, ready to go and De la Plata will be there to stop me."

"With at least a couple of dozen men to back him up."

"And riding straight into ambush. Here, let me show you."

He found a stick and drew a crude plan in a patch of damp sand. "I'll be outside the porch waiting to go, with the image on a handcart I've borrowed from Moreno. I'll have the Thompson and two or three Mills bombs handy."

Strange what tricks the mind plays on us. For a moment, this might have been one of a hundred similar jobs I had planned and undertaken over the long dark years.

"What about Janos?"

"In the bell tower, same as yesterday, with the other Thompson. You'll be on the other side of the square." He indicated the spot on his plan. "There is a broken-down stable there, no longer used by anyone. I've been up there tonight and left you the Winchester and three Mills bombs under an old sack in the right-hand corner by the loft door."

"What kind of a field of fire?"

"Couldn't be better. Forty yards from the stable to the church. I paced it out. You can't miss from the loft door at that range. They'll ride straight into the cross-fire."

I thought about it for a while, but could find no real flaws beyond the usual one that you could never depend on anything in this life, which meant that something unexpected was almost certain to happen.

"One thing," I said. "I'll be firing in your general direction. I hope you realise that."

"Son, I'll be inside that porch so fast you'll wonder if I was ever there in the first place."

A fine, light-hearted attitude. I said, "It's funny, but you had Janos and me worried back there at the church when you threw down the gauntlet to De la Plata. We thought you might be taking your role a little too seriously."

He seemed genuinely astonished, then laughed harshly. "Sure I take it seriously, Keogh. Fifty-three thousand dollars' worth."

I could have taken him up on that, because in a way, he was protesting too much, but I had no choice for Nachita appeared from the cottonwoods like some grey ghost. Even allowing for his usual impassivity, I sensed there was something.

"What is it?"

"We have a visitor, señor. For you, Father," he added, turning to van Horne. "The Señorita de la Plata."

A night for surprises.

She stood holding the bridle of her horse just beyond the firelight. One could not see much of her face, but she seemed calm enough at first when she spoke. "Forgive me, Father, but I had to speak with you. I saw Señor Janos at the hotel who thought you might be here."

Van Horne took the reins from her and handed them to Nachita. "What can I do for you?"

Her voice was still calm when she said, "Father, I know my brother and I can tell you this. He and his men will be at the church in the morning at the time you have indicated. If he finds you there he will kill you. Nothing is more certain."

Van Horne took her hands and was obviously about to reply when she cracked wide open and stumbled against him as if for support.

"Help me, Father. In pity's name, help me. I can no longer carry this dreadful burden alone."

He glanced over his shoulder at the three of us, hesitated fractionally, then led her to the tent and they went inside.

For quite some time there was bitter, agonised weeping, which finally subsided, to be followed by the low murmur of voices. It was strangely embarrassing, as if one were eavesdropping on something essentially private. We squatted by the fire without talking and drank the bitter coffee Victoria provided.

It must have been at least half-an-hour before the tent flap was thrown back and they emerged, Chela de la Plata first. She avoided my eye rather obviously and hurried to where Nachita had tethered her horse to a tree.

Van Horne went after her and she turned and asked for a blessing. He responded without the slightest hesitation, the words clear on the night air as his fingers traced the sign of the cross.

"Benedicat te Omnipotens Deus, Pater, et Filius, et Spiritus Sanctus."

She mounted and galloped away and he stayed there looking after her. I moved to his side, but before I could speak, he said, "I expect you and Janos to be in position by nine in the morning, just in case. No need to meet again before then."

He actually started to walk away and I grabbed his sleeve. "Just a minute, what was it all supposed to be about?"

"You heard, she came to warn me."

"Not that, I mean the other business."

"She had a lot on her mind. She hadn't spoken to a priest in a long time, that's all."

I said, "Are you trying to tell me you confessed her?"

He turned on me, eyes starting from his head and grabbed me by the lapel. "Does the thought amuse you, Keogh? What was I supposed to do? Say no?"

If ever I have looked at a soul in torment it was then. He pushed me away and snarled, "Anyway, what's the odds. We could all be dead by nine-thirty-five in the morning."

I watched him walk away, clear in the moonlight. For some reason I was filled with the most terrible feeling of desolation I have ever known. But no, that isn't quite true. I had known it once and once only. A century or more before. The square at Drumdoon in the rain, my brother dead before me.

I went and lay on the blankets in the tent, staring into the dark and after a while, Victoria brought me a warm drink which obviously contained a sleeping draught of some description, for within minutes of taking it, I was asleep.

THIRTEEN

I surfaced to the patter of rain against the canvas, the dim grey light of the old tent and lay there for a while, staring up at the ridge pole, relaxed and comfortable until I tried to stretch my arms and found that I could not.

For a moment, it was as if I was still asleep and dreaming, but I was very much awake as I realised when I kicked out frantically and discovered that I was bound hand and foot. I tried shouting, but after a while, the tent flap was pulled aside and Nachita ducked in. He crouched over me, his face grave.

"Where is she?" I demanded.

"Gathering wood by the stream, señor." I tried to sit up and he shook his head. "You will not go to Mojada this morning. She will not have it."

I tried to stay calm. "What time is it?"

"A little before nine, señor."

"For God's sake, Nachita, you must release me."

There was no sense in pleading for he simply got up and went out again. There wasn't much left to do after that except pull the blankets away, which was easily enough done, for my hands were tied at the front, presumably because she had wanted to hurt me as little as possible.

I barged through the tent flap head-down, falling
on my face. They had rigged up an old tarpaulin from
the tent to a couple of poles, the fire underneath and
rain ran off the edge in a steady stream. Beyond, a
heavy mist rolled down from the peaks reducing visibility considerably.

I tried to sit up and Nachita turned from the fire
and gave me a hand under my elbow, putting my back
against the saddle. At the same moment Victoria appeared from the trees, a bundle of branches in her
arms. She wore an old blanket coat and a straw sombrero against the rain.

"What in the hell are you trying to prove?" I demanded.

She dropped the branches on the ground, knelt
down and started to feed the fire without replying.

"You found your tongue again last night, or had
you forgotten?" I leaned forward. "Answer me, you
bitch."

Nachita's hand caught me across the mouth. She
moved as quickly, getting between us and pushing him
away. Her speech was slow and careful, the voice a
little remote. "Your friend dies this morning, this is
certain."

"But not me, is that it?"

Nachita was on his feet, rifle ready. He was too late.
Horses splashed through the stream, riders pouring
out of the trees to surround the camp, at least thirty of
them. I recognised two or three faces although Jurado
was conspicuous by his absence and then the line
parted and Tomás de la Plata rode through.

He was dressed as usual with the addition of a cavalry officer's caped greatcoat open down the front, presumably so that he could get to his gun if needs be.

He stared down at me for a moment, a frown on his

face, and then dismounted and squatted on his heels before me. "So, a reluctant suitor, Señor Keogh? This is not what I was told."

"She thinks I'll stand by the priest and get my head blown off if she doesn't keep me here," I told him.

"Indeed." He glanced at Victoria, then Nachita and returned to me. "She could have a point. Gringos stick together, an undeniable fact of life."

"All right, so I don't want to see the man die. He's an American citizen remember? Kill him and there could well be a lot of political pressure to have something done about it."

"His own choice, not mine."

"Then set me free and I'll persuade him otherwise."

"But I do not want you to." He seemed surprised. "Why should I? If he wishes to martyr himself, I'll be happy to accommodate him."

I still had to play my part, to react as he might reasonably expect the person I was supposed to be to react. "But why? What can there possibly be in it for you?"

He waved a hand in a gesture that sent everyone back a few yards, then leaned towards me. "Have you ever considered that when Christ rode into Jerusalem, the authorities were compelled to act as they did? Had no choice? You see, it was impossible for them to exist side-by-side. A contradiction in terms."

All this, he delivered in tones of the utmost seriousness and with a perfectly grave face. I had felt from the first there was a streak of madness in the man. Now I was certain of it.

"An interesting parallel," I said.

"Remarkably exact. How could a man like me exist in Father van Horne's world or he in mine? I would have no reality and that would be impossible, for I truly do exist as all men know, which means this priest of yours should already be dead."

I did not need that twisted logic to confirm me in the impression of a man who had definitely gone over the edge of things, for I saw nothing but madness in his eyes as he stood up.

He produced a gold hunter from inside his coat and flicked it open. "You will excuse me now, but in exactly twelve minutes I have an appointment and I like to be on time." He swung into the saddle and pulled in his horse which trampled through the fire, upsetting the coffeepot. "I am sorry to leave you like this, my friend. Someone should have warned you that you were playing with fire. Let us hope this little barbarian here keeps her knife in her belt."

He cantered away into the mist, his men following him and I turned to Victoria and said desperately, "Release me now, I beg you, while there is still time."

She started to turn away so I did the only thing left to me, which was to drop forward on my knees and thrust my bound wrists into the scattered embers of the fire. The pain was unbelievable and I was unable to restrain a groan, but she was already on me, dragging me back against the saddle.

I said, "You have nothing to gain—everything to lose. Do you think that we could ever live together after a betrayal like this? That I could look at you and not remember?"

The great dark eyes widened and I knew that I had struck deep. She wavered, genuine pain in her eyes and I pushed my hands out towards her. "Anything later than now is no good."

It worked. Her hand went inside the blanket coat and came out clutching a knife so sharp that she was through the rope in one easy slice. As she repeated the

performance on my ankles, Nachita emerged from the
tent and handed me the Enfield in its shoulder holster.
I struggled into the straps and said, "I'll be too late
at the main gate. Is there another way?"

"The wall crumbles at the top of the village near
the church, señor. Easy to climb. I could show you."

He glanced enquiringly at her as he said this and
she nodded. I grabbed her hand as she turned away,
pulled her round and smiled. "Believe it or not, but I
intend to come back."

But she didn't believe me, not for a moment, I could
tell as much from her eyes. To be honest, I wasn't too
confident myself considering the way things were going.

I took the nearest horse bare-back, with nothing but
a rope halter to hang on to, putting my heels into him
hard and galloped into the mist, urging him on with
a clenched fist.

Nachita was beside me in an instant, drawing abreast
to lead the way, riding magnificently, his old rifle in
one hand. We went headlong through rough broken
ground that had my heart in my mouth, turned into a
deep arroyo with a few inches of rain water in the
bottom, scrambled up a steep bank at the other end
and emerged into the open no more than twenty or
thirty yards from the wall at the top end of the village.

I could see what he meant at once for in places the
adobe brick had crumbled, reducing the height to
about ten feet. I pushed my horse against the wall,
stood on its back and Nachita crowded his horse in
beside me to hold things steady for a moment. My
height, as always, was the trouble. I was perhaps a
foot short, but a quick jump took care of that and the

gaps between the crumbling brick made excellent footholds.

I gave Nachita a quick wave and dropped straight over the other side into a small courtyard. There was a door in the far wall which proved to be unlocked. I opened it and found myself in a narrow alley that emptied into the square no more than a couple of steps away.

When I peered round the corner I found I was perhaps forty yards from the church. The cart van Horne had mentioned was in position a couple of yards in front of the porch and had been covered by some kind of brightly covered blanket or tapestry. The image of St. Martin de Porres stood on it in solitary splendour. There was no sign of van Horne and Janos, too, was keeping well out of sight for I could see nothing of him in the bell tower.

Somewhere I heard horses trampling over the cobbles on their way up to the village and it came to me then that this building here on the corner must be the stable van Horne had referred to.

A flight of stone stairs led up from the street through a wooden door. When I opened it, the loft door van Horne had mentioned stood wide giving a clear view of the church and a porch. I saw that he was standing inside, presumably sheltering from the rain.

I found the sacking in the corner as he had described, the Winchester and the Mills bombs, ready primed, I was pleased to see. I was barely in time for as I returned to the loft door, De la Plata's men emerged from the left in a solid bunch, wheeled and turned to face the porch in a ragged line.

It couldn't have been more perfect. I was aware of many things in that final moment. Tomás de la Plata himself in the cavalry greatcoat. Van Horne moving into the entrance of the porch in full regalia, including a superb gold cope, presumably in honour of the occasion.

I picked up a grenade, pulling the pin with my teeth and got ready to throw it, and in the same moment a rider thundered out of the street into the square, pulling in the horse so sharply between van Horne and Tomás that it slipped on the wet cobbles and slid back into its haunches.

Chela de la Plata, arriving too late, for van Horne was already bringing the Thompson round from behind his back and firing and a grenade sailed down from the bell tower to explode in exactly the right spot to take care of half-a-dozen men and their mounts in one breath.

I lobbed mine in for good measure with a similar result for the woman was dead. Had to be. I caught a glimpse of her, the face drenched in blood, her brother beside her, trying to hold her in the saddle and then they went down together, horses and all, as Janos leaned out of the bell tower and started to work the other Thompson gun from side-to-side.

It was a bad mistake for they were firing back by now and suddenly, he stopped shooting and leaned across the windowsill, head down. Very slowly, pulled by his immense weight, he simply squeezed through and followed the Thompson to the cobbles twenty feet below.

During this time I had fired continuously, choosing each target carefully and had picked off four of them with complete certainty. In spite of all this, several riders had passed below me to make good their escape through the alley to my right.

The square was heavy with smoke, the cries of the

dying, the animals, and for a while, it was impossible to see clearly. There was a sudden rush, I got the Winchester to my shoulder and lowered it as a bunch of riderless horses thundered out of the murk, crowding towards the alley.

Too late, I saw the leg hooked over one in the centre, recognised the fluttering cape of the cavalry greatcoat. I caught one quick glimpse of Tomás de la Plata glaring up at me, blood on his face, and then he and the horses were into the alley and away.

A shot chipped the jamb of the door beside my head, fired by someone still active down there. I fired back at the flash and was rewarded by a scream. There was a momentary silence, the roll of the Thompson, then silence again.

After a while, van Horne called, "Are you there, Keogh? It's all over."

I reloaded the Winchester on the way down and went to meet him, pausing to put a bullet in the head of a horse that rolled on its side with the stomach showing.

Van Horne emerged from the smoke and mist, the Thompson ready, still wearing his robes and that magnificent gold cope. "Janos is dead," he said. "And I can't see De la Plata."

"He got away," I told him. "Several of them made it past me into a rear alley, which I can only presume would bring them out at the bottom of the village near the main gate. The other Thompson gun would have done better work here."

"No sense in crying over spilt milk," he said. "I thought we had him, but it was only his horse. His sister was something I didn't foresee."

His voice was quite hoarse and he seemed to find difficulty in speaking for he suddenly pushed the Thomp-

son into my hands, turned and walked away. I followed in time to see him take off the gold cope and
spread it over the woman's body, then he went into
the church.

I retrieved the other Thompson which Janos had
dropped from the tower, checked that it still worked,
then started down the main street, a Thompson in
each hand. I found Moreno and a handful of others
outside the hotel, as frightened a bunch of men as I
have ever seen.

He hurried towards me. "Father van Horne, he is
all right?"

I nodded. "How many rode out through the gate?
Did you see?"

"Six, señor, and Don Tomás was one of them, riding
like a madman, blood on his face."

"His sister tried to stop it happening," I said. "And
got killed instead."

"Mother of God." He crossed himself as did several
of those with him. "You put Jesus in my mouth,
señor. We will all die for this day's work."

"Not if you have any guts left. Guns and ammunition aplenty on the ground outside the church if you
rob the dead. In the meantime, I'd put a couple
of men on the wall by the main gate if I were you.
They can have the machine guns, not that I think
they'll be needed, but it pays to take care. There's a
Lieutenant Cordona with a cavalry detachment at the
old *rancheria* at Huanca. He'll come galloping to the
rescue if you get a message off to him."

He took a deep breath and nodded. "You are right,
señor, panic is of no assistance in such a situation. At
least two dozen people ran out into the open country
in blind terror when the shooting started. You must

understand we have seen some terrible things in these parts over the years. Whole villages slaughtered—women, children. One would think God had turned his back on Mexico."

I managed to cut him off at that point, showed the two men he selected how to pull the trigger on the machine guns and left them all to it.

I had the bar to myself, found a bottle of scotch and poured a large one. God, what a mess. All that killing, the girl dead and Tomás de la Plata still ran free. I was suddenly sick of the whole business, sick and angry at the world, but most of all with van Horne.

I went back up the street to the square where Moreno and his men already moved amongst the dead and entered the church. Van Horne was sitting on a bench at the front near the altar still wearing his alb. He didn't even turn his head as I went up the aisle.

I stopped beside him and he said, "Don't say it, Keogh, I know."

Standing there looking down at him, all the anger and frustration evaporated. The truth at last and facing up to it carried its own release.

"No, you don't," I said. "My fault as well as yours. Everything that's happened and we can always include the good Colonel Bonilla and Tomás de la Plata."

"Collective responsibility?" he said gravely. "Not really good enough. In the final analysis, a man must accept personal responsibility for his own actions."

"Which sounds as if it could have come straight out of the middle section of some theology lecture at that seminary of yours," I said.

"Very possibly."

He was unable to take the conversation any further

for Moreno called from the doorway. "Come quickly, Father."

When we went out of the porch, I found Nachita on the ground against the wall. He looked half stunned, blood oozing from a contusion on the right of his forehead.

I dropped to one knee and he grabbed my coat. "He sent me, señor. The Evil One himself sent me."

I knew instantly what had happened, saw it all in one terrible moment of truth, yet things had to have their logical sequence.

"He has Victoria?"

He nodded. "And twenty-one other people, señor. Villagers from this place. Some only children."

The ones who had run into the open country in panic.

"What does he want?" van Horne demanded harshly.

"You, Father," Nachita said. "He just wants you. No one else. He gives you two hours."

FOURTEEN

Inside the church away from the others, Nachita filled in the unpleasant facts. Tomás de la Plata had only five men left, it was true, but they were ample for his purpose. On the other side of the stream there was an abandoned *casa*, only the walls still standing and he had his hostages penned in there. The slightest sign of an attack and they died instantly.

The effect of all this on van Horne was considerable. The flesh seemed to have withered on his bones if such a thing were possible, the face itself to have sunk in so that he looked old and tired and past everything there ever was.

He turned without a word and went down to the vestry. I left Nachita and followed him. He had a whisky bottle in one hand, a glass in the other. His hand shook quite distinctly as he poured. He tossed the whisky back in one mouthful and had another.

"God dammit, Keogh, what are we going to do?"

"I don't know," I said. "It needs thinking about."

He brightened suddenly, probably the first quick effects of the alcohol. "We could have a go. You, me and the Indian. He'd come with us. We could take them, Keogh, between us. He's only got five to back him up now, remember."

"We wouldn't even get close," I said. "One shot,

that's all it would take and he'd kill the lot of them."

He turned on me angrily. "How in the hell can you be certain? You haven't even been to take a look at the situation. Perfect cover in this mist and rain."

He was talking into the wind, we both knew that. I said, "Let's go down to the gate and look things over."

He pulled off his alb, found his shovel hat and we went out through the church. The surprise came when I opened the door to the porch.

Bad news spreads faster than the plague. I should think that virtually every living soul in the village stood there waiting in the heavy rain. Dark, anxious faces, not a sound, no open mourning. A despairing acceptance of the whole terrible business as a fact of life.

For a moment, they confronted each other, as it were, van Horne and the crowd and then a strange thing happened, infinitely beautiful, yet terrible in its way.

An old woman and a young girl stood together at the front, the girl clutching a bundle wrapped in a cloth, her thin blouse saturated, clinging to her breasts, outlining them perfectly. I remember this clearly and the great sorrow in her eyes as the old woman gave her a push forward.

The girl offered the bundle to van Horne who took it instinctively. She said simply, "Candles, Father, for the dead."

She went down on her knees in front of him and most of the crowd followed suit. There was a kind of tableau there, the kneeling people, the heavy rain rushing into the ground, van Horne looking down at the girl, the bundle in one hand.

He raised her up and when he spoke, his voice was

calm, gentle, the most wonderful smile on his face. "Come inside, child, out of the rain. All of you, come inside."

It was as if I had ceased to exist for him for he turned and went back into the church without a word for me. I got out of the way and Nachita, who had been standing against the wall, joined me. Most of those present had probably not been inside a church for years and yet they were calm and orderly about it as they went in, the women covering their heads.

Nachita said, "What do they intend to do in there, señor, pray for a miracle?"

"I suppose so."

He shook his head. "I have no faith in such things. Neither does Tomás de la Plata."

My own sentiments exactly and I turned and we went down through the village together to the main gate.

Visibility was not much more than fifty or sixty yards, so heavy was the rain. They had closed the gates, barring them securely, so I went up on the wall to see what I could see, which was precisely nothing.

Nachita came up a little later with an old blanket poncho he had picked up from somewhere and a palm-woven sombrero. I put them on though I was wet enough already and stared out into an alien land.

I said, "Is there anything we can do?"

He shook his head. "The first sign of a move against him and they die."

I tried to think of Victoria and the rest of them out there beyond the stream in the old *casa* and found it an impossibility, even when I tried to concentrate on her alone. I was cold, chilled through to the centre of things, soaking wet under the old poncho, the straps of my shoulder holster rubbing painfully.

There was a curiously dreamlike flavour to it all. It was as if it could not really be happening. As if I might wake up at any moment, but to what, that was the thing.

"There is nothing to be done, then?" I said. "Is that what you are saying?"

"There is the priest, señor."

I moved away from the man who guarded this side of the gate with one of the Thompsons and Nachita followed me. I said, "He is not a priest. Not a real priest. You know this."

"It does not matter, señor. He is what De la Plata wants and I will not stand by and see my lady die."

"He might kill them all anyway," I said. "Have you thought of that?"

A shot sounded through the rain, out there in the mist somewhere and the guard on our side fired a burst in panic. Nachita grabbed his arm to stay him and we listened in the silence.

"Hello, the wall!" a voice called. "No shooting."

We waited and a man emerged from the mist, one of the villagers, his hands tied before him, a halter around his neck. The horseman on the other end was Raul Jurado.

"Señor Keogh," he called. "Don Tomás presents his compliments to the priest. He has till twelve-thirty. This is to show him we mean business."

He released the rope, the wretched man on the other end broke into a shambling run. Jurado shot him twice in the back and was into the cover of the mist in an instant.

I passed people coming down the street as I went up to the church. When I went inside, there were still a few sitting quietly on the benches. I paused uncertainly and Moreno came out of the side-chapel clutching his sombrero in both hands.

I said, "Where is Father van Horne?"

"In the chapel, señor, hearing confessions. For most people here it has been a very long time."

I brushed past him and went down towards the altar, pausing in the entrance of the tiny side-chapel. The image of St. Martin de Porres stood in a niche in the wall. Van Horne sat on a bench below and the woman before him was just getting to her knees.

He'd said something to her quickly, got up and came towards me. He was wearing the alb again over his cassock, a violet stole round his shoulders and his calm was remarkable when one sonsidered the state he'd been in earlier.

He said in a low voice, "Is it urgent, Keogh? I'm rather busy."

I took him by the arm, drew him along to the other end of the church and told him what had just happened. He listened gravely, then took out his watch. "That gives us an hour and a quarter."

"And no time to be wasting in this sort of bloody charade."

"They've had a lot to put up with, poor devils. A little comfort won't come amiss at this stage."

"A little comfort is it?" I pulled the purple stole from around his neck. "Don't you know what this stands for? Don't you realise what you are doing?"

"Whatever wrong in this business is mine, not theirs." He smiled sombrely. "I must say that for a man who does not believe in God, the fact of sin seems to weigh heavily on you."

"You go to hell," I said and tossed the stole in his face.

"I very probably will, Keogh." He laughed harshly, his old self again for a brief moment. "Does that thought give you any kind of satisfaction?"

"This kind of thing wasn't in the contract," I said. "It goes entirely too far. All right, in other circumstances it might just be acceptable. A priest, after all, is still a priest, whatever he has done. Whatever he has become."

"Exactly," he said gravely.

I stared at him, the full implication of what he was saying taking its own time to sink in. And yet it was as if I had always known from the first and at every point that followed. Sensed that he was not even the two people I had thought him, that he had alternated between. He was someone else. A different man altogether.

He put a hand on my shoulder as if to speak, but I recoiled in horror, turned and rushed out into the rain.

When I went into the bar at the hotel, Moreno was behind the bar polishing glasses in a mechanical way, his eyes staring into space. He pulled himself together quickly and produced a bottle of whisky and a glass.

"You saw the good father, señor?" he asked as he filled the glass. "A wonderful man. There can be few like him."

"True enough," I replied and drank my whisky.

"A man who can work miracles. It is no exaggeration to claim this, señor."

"A point of view," I said. "And what do you think he'll manage to pull out of his hat for the hostages?"

"Señor?" He stared at me, a puzzled frown on his face.

"Will he let them die?" I demanded. "Or will

he make the final sacrifice? It's an interesting thought,
you must agree."

His eyes widened in horror. "Oh, no, señor, never
that. It would be inconceivable."

He turned as if I were the Devil himself and rushed
out. In the silence following, van Horne said from behind me, "You would seem to have upset him."

"He believes you to be Christ walking the earth
again," I said.

For a moment, the old anger rumbled in his voice.
"Dammit, Keogh, but it's easy to see that the Jesuits
schooled you."

I raised a hand. "All right, point taken."

"Good, then will you listen for a while? I haven't
got long and for some reason I find it important to
come to some understanding with you."

He produced one of his cigarillos, lit it and sat at
the nearest table. "To start with, my name isn't van
Horne. What it is, no longer matters either to me or
anyone else. I told you I spent four years in a seminary
and walked out."

"Another lie?"

"The story of my life." The old humour again. "Five
years, Keogh. Five years and ordination at the end of
it."

I stared down into my glass, the significance of what
he had said drifting through to me. "It's funny," he
said. "But looking back on it all now, I realise that I
never really wanted it, that was the trouble. And when
I walked out, the girl I thought I was in love with was
only an excuse. A convenient peg to hang the blame
on ever since."

I took the bottle and my glass and slumped down
at the table opposite him. "I'm sorry," I said. "I don't

know what to say except that it occurs to me that I am the last person in the world to have the right to throw stones at you."

"Have you ever thought of going home?" he asked.

"To Ireland?" I shrugged. "They'd shoot me on sight."

"Oh, I don't know. This civil war of yours is bound to finish sooner or later. They'll offer some sort of amnesty. They usually do. You could go back to the university. Finish that final year of medical training."

"A pipe-dream," I said. "It could never be now."

"You mean the girl?" He nodded. "You could have a point. You'd be asking a lot to expect her to find roots in such an alien culture."

"In the right clothes, you wouldn't be able to tell the difference between her and half the girls in Kerry," I said. "No, I mean more than that. You once told me I had death in the soul and you were right. I've walked in dark places for too long to change."

"I don't agree," he said. "A man is personally responsible for what he is, Keogh. He's what he wants to be and change is always possible and entirely in his own hands. If you never remember anything else I ever said to you, remember that."

He reached for the bottle and my glass. "One for the road," he said, filling the glass and took the whisky back in one quick swallow.

"What do you mean?"

"Once a priest, always a priest, Keogh. You know that, whatever kind of Catholic you are and so do I. I've done everything wrong that's possible, but that doesn't matter. There's no escape. Never has been."

He got to his feet and moved to the door. "You mean you're going out there?"

"I've no choice," he said calmly. "I never had and not because I've suddenly turned holy at the end of things."

"What, then?"

"Pride, Keogh, foolish pride. I've played my part too well. These people believe in me. More than that— trust in me. I can't break the image now."

I caught him by the sleeve as he opened the door. "Not a single person has asked you to go—right?"

"The final nail in my coffin, boy."

He pulled himself free, went outside and stood at the top of the steps. The street was full of people again, a repetition of that earlier scene outside the church. The people were waiting and the people knew, could sense what was to happen. It showed on their faces.

As he went down the steps, they started to drop to their knees and he blessed them as he walked towards the gate. I followed at his heels. Moreno stood with his back to the gate, his hat in his hands.

Van Horne said, "Open it, my friend."

Moreno dropped to his knees, weeping bitterly.

Van Horne turned quietly to me and for the first and only time called me by my Christian name. "It takes two hands if you've got them, Emmet."

It was as if it had all happened before and perhaps this explains the strange inevitability I felt. I walked to the gates, lifted the bar without opening them and felt his hand on my shoulder.

"I once said I'd pray for you, back there in my play-acting days. I would ask you to do the same for me now, and mean it. You more than anyone else."

I was past speech, turned, clenching my teeth hard to hold back what was inside me and opened the gates. He moved a yard outside and peered into the rain.

Nothing seemed to live out there. He turned and looked at me again.

"If I never did anything else for you, accept this now. You did not kill your brother, Keogh. It was life itself and people and that bloody little war you were having just like everyone else. Believe that and start living again. Don't waste your time on De la Plata. He's already damned. Now get that gate closed and God bless you."

He turned and walked away into the rain and mist and I did as I was told.

The hostages knocked on the gate within twenty minutes and streamed inside, many of them in considerable distress. Victoria was not amongst them. At first I could not believe it and ran through the crowd, pulling people apart as they embraced, searching everywhere.

I finally came face-to-face with Nachita and the fire in his eyes confirmed my worst fears. "She is not here, señor. He has not kept his word."

I turned and found a peon standing at my side, clutching his sombrero nervously. "Señor Keogh, I have a message from Don Tomás. He was most insistent . . ."

"Go on, damn you!" I shouted.

"He said that he was keeping what you value most to remember you by. He told me to say he hopes you rest content at night thinking of them."

I stood there, staring at him in the rain, caught by the enormity of it, and from somewhere beyond the wall, Jurado's voice floated out of the mist.

"Señor Keogh!"

I ran to the gate, Nachita at my back and peered outside.

"Don Tomás sends you your friend. He wanted to play the Christian. It seemed reasonable, therefore, to allow him to die like one."

There was a single shot and a horse galloped out of the rain, plunging in fright, circling in confusion before the gate.

Van Horne had been strapped upright in the saddle against a crude wooden cross, arms outstretched, blood soaking through the front of the old cassock.

I grabbed for the reins to steady the horse and looked up at him. I suddenly realised that he was still alive. He tried to speak to me and no one else. Tried with everything he had and failed. The eyes rolled upwards, the head turned to one side.

As the sound of Jurado's horse faded into the distance, Nachita came out through the gate like a whirlwind, mounted on the first horse that had come to hand and went after him.

Not that it mattered. Not that anything seemed to have any reality any longer as the crowd surged out through the gate, strangely silent. They watched quietly as Moreno took a knife to the ropes binding van Horne and willing hands caught the body as it tumbled from the saddle.

Moreno turned to me, his eyes sad, no longer weeping. "He could have lived, señor, but chose to die instead. For us—for the people. Is not this a most remarkable thing? A saint walked amongst us and we did not recognise him."

FIFTEEN

All I could do now was wait for Nachita for there was certainly nothing to be gained by riding out into the rain myself. I went up to my room, stripped and rubbed myself down, then changed into dry clothes. I put a box of .45 cartridges into each pocket, went downstairs to the bar and helped myself to some more of Moreno's whisky while I stripped and cleaned the Enfield.

After a while Moreno himself appeared, removing his hat in a very respectful manner. "Señor, there are things at the church which belonged to him. We are not sure what to do. You were his friend . . ."

"All right," I said. "I'll come up to the church with you."

I put the poncho and sombrero back on for the rain was still falling heavily and we left the hotel and started up the street. A couple of carts, pulled by mules, passed us on the way down carrying the bodies of De la Plata's men.

"They lived without God, we shall bury them without God," Moreno explained. "The same hole does for all."

"And Señorita de la Plata also?"

"Señor, please." He looked genuinely shocked. "She, we will bury with all due ceremony. There is her father to consider, though God alone knows what the news of her death will do to that poor old man."

When we went into the square they were harnessing mules to the dead horses, getting ready to drag them off. Most of the blood had already been washed away by the heavy rain. Life continued.

Inside the church, there was a remarkable change. The benches had been moved to the sides, but a crude wooden coffin with the lid on had been laid across two of them near the entrance.

"Doña Chela, señor," Moreno murmured. "It was thought desirable to cover her now. She had been shot in the face. You understand?"

I did, all too well, and moved on to the other end of the church which was a blaze of candles.

When I first landed in Mexico I saw a procession of the Virgin through the streets of Veracruz. It was one of the most beautiful images I had ever seen except that it had a knife in the heart, which seemed to sum up Mexico admirably and the general preoccupation with death.

Van Horne lay on a table in full regalia, the gold cope over all, his hands folded around a crucifix, candles at his head and feet. He looked as if he might open his eyes at any moment.

"There was no coffin big enough to hold him, señor," Moreno whispered. "The village carpenter is already at work."

The stench of the candles was overpowering and there was nothing here for me. I had already said goodbye. I went into the vestry and Moreno followed me. The things he had spoken of were not really van Horne's. They were from the trunk that had belonged to the priest who had died at Huerta and yet I could not say so.

I said, "Keep these in a safe place. The new priest may have a use for them."

"The new priest, señor?"

"They'll send somebody, especially now that things have changed."

"And Don Tomás?"

"Is finished."

I couldn't face the church again and left the vestry by the other door, going straight down to the gates. Just as we reached the hotel, one of the guards fired a warning shot and called that a rider was coming.

I moved out through the gates with Moreno, a few more backing him up with rifles from the square. Nachita rode out of the mist, Jurado stumbling along behind, hands tied, a halter around his neck, just like the poor devil he had killed earlier.

"He couldn't run fast enough," Nachita said.

"What about the others?"

"Already gone, leaving this one to deliver the priest. The rain makes tracking difficult."

Jurado's face was still badly bruised, one eye half closed, but there was nothing but hate showing. "All right, Keogh, you've got me, but Don Tomás has your girl friend and by the time he and the boys have had their way with her . . ."

I gave him my hand across the jaw. "You can cut that out for a start. Where are they making for?"

He spat in my face. I wiped it away with the edge of my poncho and knocked him flat on his back.

Nachita said, "I could make him talk, señor."

"How long?" I said.

"No longer than it takes to light a fire."

"Then roast it out of the bastard. The sooner, the better."

And it worked, for there had never been much to

Raul Jurado except brute strength and ignorance. He
had broken in my two hands once before. He broke
now.

Nachita put heels to his horse, the halter tightening,
dragging Jurado over the rough ground and he cried
out, fear in his voice. "No, not the Indian."

Remembering some of the things Janos had told me
about the Yaqui I was not particularly surprised. I
said, "I'll only ask you once. How many men has De
la Plata got with him?"

"Five."

"Where have they gone?"

"Poneta."

I glanced at Nachita who nodded. "I know this
place. Perhaps twenty-five miles from here on the other side of the Valley of the Angels. No one has lived
there for many years now."

I nudged Jurado in the ribs with my boot. "Is he
right?"

He nodded sullenly. "Don Tomás has used the place
often in the past. From there, he can send into
the mountains for men."

It had the ring of truth, so I dragged him to his feet
and shoved him in the general direction of Moreno
and his friends. "Keep him for the *federales,*" I said.
"Let them do it the legal way."

He turned, cursing me, but Moreno slapped his face.
A couple of them grabbed hold of the end of the halter
and they all moved back into the village, dragging him
along behind.

Nachita dismounted and we followed them. "This
place, Poneta," I said. "What's it like?"

"A ruined church on the edge of a ravine, three or
four streets. It was a government strong point in the
early days of the Revolution. The scene of much

heavy fighting. Most of the inhabitants were killed. The few that survived went elsewhere."

We turned into the courtyard at the rear of the hotel where I had parked the Mercedes. I found the map Bonilla had given us and unfolded it across the driver's seat out of the rain, for the canvas hood was up.

"How long would it take us to get there?"

"Five or six hours, señor. A little more, a little less, depending on the horses. The Valley of the Angels is twenty miles wide. All desert, no water. A place in which to take care."

"What start would you say they have on us?"

"An hour—an hour and a half."

"Could we catch them before they reach Poneta?"

"Perhaps, if we took spare horses, but he would kill her the moment we appeared."

I looked at the map again, particularly the wide desert area of the Valley of the Angels and the solution seemed plain. "What if we got there first? What if we were waiting for them?"

"Señor?" He frowned. "But how could such a thing be?"

I tapped the driving wheel of the Mercedes. "In this," I said, "All things are possible."

It was the first time I had seen him smile.

It was something of an emotional leave-taking. Moreno was reluctant to let us go, having dispatched a rider to Cordona at Huanca and inclining to the opinion that I should await the lieutenant's arrival.

Before I got into the Mercedes, he gave me the *abrazo,* the formal hug, patting me on the back, tears in his eyes, convinced, I suppose, that he would never see me alive again. Even so, it was interesting to note that not a single individual offered to accompany us, which

all made Moreno's parting *Go with God* sound a little
hollow as we drove away.

I was glad to put Mojada behind me for many reasons and I think I knew then that I would never see
the place again, nor did I want to.

At the final end of things, whatever else he had
been, Oliver van Horne had died for people who
weren't even prepared to help themselves. One could
find excuses in plenty for them. The wretchedness of
their lives, the years of suffering which, in the end, had
come to seem the natural order of things. But the end
result was still that they would not help themselves.
Would not move a finger to help anyone else.

I was filled with a feeling of indescribable bitterness.
I was sick of them and I was sick of this festering land
they called a country. The anger in me took control so
that I went over the crown of the pass at a speed that
was excessive under the conditions.

As we went down, the rain slackened and the mist
thinned considerably and then the track petered out
into a shallow slope running into the bottom of the
great valley, dotted with mesquite and cactus trees. We
went down past a tangle of catclaw and brush over
tilted slabs and emerged to a flat plain of hard-baked
sand.

I braked to a halt and Nachita got out and scouted
around in wide circles. It didn't take long and he returned quickly. "They have passed this way, as I expected. The tracks are plain."

The old trail was clearly marked on the military
map. Straight across, which was naturally the shortest
route, and there was Poneta half-way up a mountain.
Twenty miles, perhaps a little less.

My own strategy was obvious. Nachita got back into

the Mercedes and I drove eastward for about five miles, hugging the edge of the desert, then turned north and drove across the hard, sun-baked earth at what to Nachita must have seemed the considerable speed of twenty-five miles an hour.

We crossed without incident, reaching the foothills of the mountains on the other side of the valley in just on the hour. I turned west and followed the rim of the desert for several miles until we came to the beginning of the track on that side, starting up through the narrow pass between two mountains exactly as indicated on the map.

I dropped into a low gear for it lifted steeply through slopes covered with mesquite and greasewood and as we climbed higher, a few scattered *piñones,* and Nachita dropped out and followed along behind, erasing the tire tracks wtih a branch from a thorn tree. The trail started to hug the side of the mountain, the slope dropping away steeply and then we crawled round a massive outcrop of rock and found Poneta perched on the edge of a ravine.

It was larger than I had supposed, must have once been reasonably important, which was to be judged mainly from the size of the church, a large, flat-roofed building in stone with a badly damaged bell tower, the result of shell fire from the look of it.

The rest of the buildings were crumbling adobe *casas,* most of them without a roof and everywhere the signs of the battle which had raged over the place.

I drove up the main street, Nachita ready with his old Winchester, but it was ours alone except for the lizards and the ravens perched on top of the crumbling bell tower, watching as I braked to a halt in the centre of the plaza by an empty fountain.

I found one of the canteens, washed the dust from my throat and passed it to Nachita. Two or three ravens lifted into the air calling hoarsely to each other. The sun died. I shivered, the Celt in me again.

"A bad place. Too many men have died here," Nachita said.

I nodded. "We'll wait for them back along the trail where we can see what's coming."

We found a *casa* on the edge of the village with one wall missing, which made it an excellent hiding place for the Mercedes as I was able to drive it right inside. We left it there and walked back down the trail to the point where it disappeared round the outcrop and climbed up to the top.

The view of the desert was excellent. Nachita beat amongst the bushes for snakes and we settled down to wait. I had one of the Thompson guns and he, his Winchester, but it was going to be difficult to attack them without harming Victoria, and her safety, after all, was what mattered. Too much was going to have to be left to chance and I had never cared for that in this kind of business.

I lay back, head pillowed on my sombrero, smoked a cigarette and narrowed my eyes into infinity, wondering in a detached sort of way how Victoria was and what she was thinking. Yet she must know that we would follow. Had no choice.

And Tomás de la Plata? Impossible to judge which way he would jump. He was a man who had endured much and had been moulded by a hundred different things. The years in prison, the degradation, the humiliations endured for the cause he believed in. The long struggle. So much killing.

Yet others had been through as much and had survived. There was something deeper here. This man had been touched in the darkest depths of him and a man like that was to be feared.

I must have drifted into sleep and Nachita had obviously decided to let me be. When he brought me awake with a quick shake, it was late evening, the valley purple with shadow, the sun an orange ball.

The clatter of hooves was quite distinct on the quiet air and I peered cautiously through the brush and saw them coming up the trail below, coated with dust from the desert, weariness in every line of them, men and beasts.

And at the end we were still out of luck for Victoria and Tomás de la Plata shared the same horse, his arms around her as he held the reins. To start anything with the girl in such a position would be madness. We lay there quietly and watched them enter the village and start up the main street to the plaza.

I said, "If I can draw them off, it's unlikely he'd leave more than one man in charge of Victoria and you could handle that."

"And how would you accomplish this thing, señor?"

I told him briefly. He said, "You go to your death, you know this?"

"Maybe it's about time." I shrugged. "Just get Victoria out of harm's way when the time comes and I mean that. She's your only consideration. Forget about me, no matter what happens."

I went down through the brush in a strangely resigned mood. I would do what had to be done and if it meant the end of me, let it be so. A long time coming, surely.

Nachita helped me roll the Mercedes silently backwards out of the ruined *casa* where we had left it, then

I climbed behind the wheel, the Thompson ready on the passenger seat beside me. The roar of that magnificent engine nearly tore the place apart as I put my foot down hard and took her up the narrow street to the plaza.

Tomás de la Plata, a hand on Victoria's arm, was crossing towards the church, his men walking behind, leading the horses. I braked to a halt, stayed that way long enough to see the shock of recognition in his face, then reversed. They had already started shooting as I took the Mercedes back into the narrow street. The windscreen shattered and I ducked instinctively, swerving enough to demolish one end of an adobe wall.

It slowed me a little, which was what I wanted anyway. The hounds were in full cry now and I kept on going, head down, bullets thudding into the bodywork of the Mercedes and then I was out of the village and into the open again.

I swung the wheel from side-to-side to make her swerve, then drove the Mercedes clear over the edge of the trail.

She went down the slope like a thunderbolt, tearing a path through the mesquite and brushwood and I grabbed the Thompson and got out while the going was good. The Mercedes bounced, turned over twice and tore into a clump of *piñón*, finally coming to rest upside down.

I lay in the brush hugging the ground and the Thompson and waited. A few moments later they appeared on the trail above, Tomás de la Plata and his men, one of them holding on to Victoria. They paused on the edge looking at the Mercedes, then De la Plata said something and started down with four of them, leaving Victoria and the man who was holding her.

Nachita appeared behind them as if out of thin air. Whatever was done, was done silently for the man went down without a cry and Nachita pulled Victoria back out of sight.

Which was all I had been waiting for. There was a crashing in the brushwood as De la Plata and his men approached and it was now or never for they were almost on me.

They emerged into a clear patch in a long straggling line and I stood up and started to fire, intending to take the five of them in one clean sweep. The first two went over like skittles and then the round drum magazine jammed.

It was De la Plata who fired in return, drawing from the shoulder holster of his with incredible speed like a snake striking, the bullet catching me just above the right breast, knocking me back into the brush.

As I hit the ground, I drew the Enfield, fired twice very fast to keep the heads down and allowed myself to slide down through the brush as fast as possible.

I fetched up in a thicket and paused long enough to examine my wound. The force of the shot had been considerable owing to the short range and the bullet had passed straight through, exiting under the right shoulder blade. The exit hole was smaller than I had anticipated which meant, in all probability, that his revolver was of .38 calibre.

I spat into my hand and produced no blood which was encouraging, but the sounds of movement in the brush above were not. I got out of the thicket quickly and started to work my way up the slope again, following a diagonal course to the right which would bring me back to the trail.

Someone caught sight of me soon enough, there was a cry and then another, three or four shots. A last mad scramble and I went over the edge of the trail, lungs bursting, to find one of them bearing down on me from the left like a steam engine.

I fired wildly twice without taking aim, for I had no choice in the matter, tripped and went headlong, crying out as the pain surged through me. The man running in did not fire, preferring to get close. It was the death of him for I shot him in the heart, the heavy bullet lifting him off his feet and back over the edge of the trail.

There was one round left in the Enfield and no time to reload. As De la Plata and his surviving companion appeared from the brush, I turned and ran for my life into the village.

They fired continuously, but thanks to that mad chase through the brush, the scramble up the slope, nobody's aim was anything to boast about. I put my head down and kept running, hoping to make it to the church, hoping that Nachita might take a hand in the game in spite of what I had said.

I had almost reached the fountain when I was hit again. The right leg this time, only a crease, but enough to bring me down.

When I rolled over, De la Plata's companion was some distance in front of him, a young man, full of his strength and running well. There was no time for fancy shooting. I simply aimed at his middle and pulled the trigger, was on my feet and scrambling for the church door as he went down.

He was like some creature in a nightmare that is impossible to shake off. I made it to the door, a bullet chipping the wall. When I glanced over my shoulder he was already past the fountain and running very fast, a pistol in each hand.

I staggered through the cool darkness inside, not daring to stop, fumbling for spare cartridges in my pocket. I managed to get two into the chamber awkwardly, dropping a few in the process because my right shoulder and arm were burning like all the fires of hell now and the fingers weren't working very well.

He was inside and shooting, uncertain in the light. Like a fool I fired back, giving myself away, turned and stumbled into the shadows as he replied.

I fell across a flight of stone steps and scrambled up them desperately. They turned a corner, the inner wall of the bell tower and light flooded down through a great jagged hole. I emerged on the roof and paused briefly to get my bearings. A bullet whined into the air through the opening. I fired down into the darkness twice in reply and the second time, the hammer clicked on nothing.

I was finished and I knew it. Little Emmet Keogh at the end of things at last, for he came up the steps without hesitation. I turned and went staggering along the roof to nowhere and when I reached the ultimate edge, there was no parapet, only a long fall down to the ravine below or the plaza on the other side.

When I turned, he was standing perhaps ten yards away, chest heaving, face very pale, a pistol in one hand only now. And in the end, he made the worst kind of mistake. Instead of shooting me out of hand, he had to talk.

"Who sent you, Keogh?"

His reply was a single shot that echoed across the roof tops sending the ravens wheeling up in dark, frightened circles. De la Plata cried out and spun round, the pistol jumping from his hand into the plaza.

Nachita was standing by the fountain, the Winchester at his shoulder, Victoria crouched beside him. She cried my name suddenly and the echo mingled with the hoarse calling of the ravens.

As I swung round, De la Plata flung himself at me blindly, blood on his mouth, hands reaching out to destroy. I simply moved to one side and he blundered over the edge into the plaza.

He was lying face-down on the cobbles when I looked, Nachita kneeling beside him. Nachita rose, glanced up at me, then turned and followed Victoria, who was running for the church door.

The ravens descended to the tower again, black against a sky the colour of brass, and the sun died behind the peaks. I was tired and the Enfield empty in my left hand was still a weight to carry. A fine dramatic gesture to toss it away once and for all, far out into space over the ravine, but that would not have been the sensible way. Not little Emmet Keogh of the left hand's way. This was a bad place to be and night falling.

I sat down, spilled the handful of cartridges beside me and slowly, and with great difficulty because of my wounded shoulder, started to reload.